The Chance of a Lifetime

Charles stepped forward with what looked like a scroll. He unraveled it to the ground, a ridiculous number of loose-leaf pages stapled end to end. "Whereas," he announced, "we th   too many t   "

"Ch

"No

"Anc   ned,
withou   est,
most t   our
school   me,
proven   one
ever se

"Her

"Her   ffer
outrigh   to
Casey (ma
Club o

They   ive
eyes.

One   e?"
Harriso

"It's t   iid.
"It's the

Begg   ith
no expe

Drama Club
Book 1:

The Fall Musical

Peter Lerangis

speak
An Imprint of Penguin Group (USA) Inc.

SPEAK

Published by the Penguin Group
Penguin Group (USA) Inc.,
345 Hudson Street, New York, New York 10014, U.S.A.
Penguin Group (Canada), 90 Eglinton Avenue East, Suite 700,
Toronto, Ontario, Canada M4P 2Y3 (a division of Pearson Penguin Canada Inc.)
Penguin Books Ltd, 80 Strand, London WC2R 0RL, England
Penguin Ireland, 25 St Stephen's Green, Dublin 2, Ireland (a division of Penguin Books Ltd)
Penguin Group (Australia), 250 Camberwell Road, Camberwell, Victoria 3124, Australia
(a division of Pearson Australia Group Pty Ltd)
Penguin Books India Pvt Ltd, 11 Community Centre,
Panchsheel Park, New Delhi - 110 017, India
Penguin Group (NZ), 67 Apollo Drive, Rosedale, North Shore 0745, Auckland, New Zealand
(a division of Pearson New Zealand Ltd.)
Penguin Books (South Africa) (Pty) Ltd, 24 Sturdee Avenue,
Rosebank, Johannesburg 2196, South Africa

Registered Offices: Penguin Books Ltd, 80 Strand, London WC2R 0RL, England

Published by Speak, an imprint of Penguin Group (USA) Inc., 2007

1 3 5 7 9 10 8 6 4 2

LIBRARY OF CONGRESS CATALOGING-IN-PUBLICATION DATA
Lerangis, Peter.
Drama club : book 1 : the fall musical / by Peter Lerangis.
p. cm.
ISBN 978-0-14-240886-5
1. High school students—Fiction. 2. Acting—Fiction. I. Title.
PS3569.I5257D73 2007
813'.54–dc22   2007015296

Speak ISBN 978-0-14-240886-5

Printed in the United States of America

To the stars that dazzle:

Tina, Nick, and Joe

Prologue

THEY SAY IF YOU STARE AT THE PHOTOS LONG enough, you'll see yourself. You can't miss them. They cover an entire wall of the school lobby, every year since 1907. The ones way up top are hard to see, but they're all boys in togas, animal skins, and drag. Often a mysterious blurry bear lurks in the background, supposedly the ghost of a murdered kid but probably some forgotten joke. It was a boys' school then, and when girls showed up a couple of decades later, the Masque & Wig Society became the Drama Club.

Every few years a newspaper will do a feature on this. They'll say most high schools have walls for sports teams, debate teams, math squads, etc. But, they'll conclude, Ridgeport High is "not most high schools." And they're right. Okay, if you look *real* hard, you'll find a small dusty cabinet near the boys' room that contains a few trophies and a list of track records intact since Lamar Williams high-jumped 6′ 1¼″ in 1985. I guess Kyle Taggart's football records will be added someday, but no one seems to be rushing (ha ha). But the lobby wall, the school's prime show-off spot, is reserved for something else, something much more important.

Ridgeport is the kind of place where Stephen Sondheim is sung in the hallways, *The Light in the Piazza* is on everyone's playlists, and you can spark a heated argument by mentioning the name Martin Pakledinaz. (He's a costume designer. I didn't know that either.) Kids give impromptu concerts in the halls, and teachers sing backup. Even Mr. Ippolito, the custodian, does a mean doo-wop second tenor and can recite Shakespeare. He keeps the photos spotless. Especially the Shrine, a glassed-in photo display of the five RHS alums who went on to win Tony Awards.

Brianna Glaser swears she was, in a previous life, the girl playing in *Annie Get Your Gun* in a 1966 photo; the girl doesn't resemble her at all, but it's hard to disagree with Brianna. Harrison Michaels is the guy playing Zeus in some 1931 play. Reese Van Cleve is, of course, the babe in 1989's *Pajama Game* with the 300-watt smile, long legs, and big boobs—a girl who, depending on who you talk to, went on to become a backup singer for Madonna or an Internet porn star.

Me? I didn't pay much attention to the photos at first. For one thing, there were no Asian faces for, oh, seventy years. Brianna insisted that didn't matter and that I was being close-minded, but I think I'm a realist. People see what they want to see. I mean, we all dream of a perfect place, where everyone *gets* you. Where you can be exactly who you want to be and not worry about making an ass of yourself or pleasing someone else. Some people find it in teams and social cliques. Some have to travel to an imaginary wizard school or through a hidden wardrobe or on a Kansas tornado. In Ridgeport, people find it in the Drama Club.

As for me, I had to work a little harder. A few weeks after I turned sixteen, in another life in Connecticut, everything changed. Nothing I knew or believed made any sense. On that day I stopped being Kara Chang. I was no longer the good girl, the Organized One, the class president and yearbook editor who could do Whatever She Put Her Mind To. After the school year ended, Mom and I moved away. We had to. Dad probably would have wanted us to stay, but he'd walked out on us three years earlier, so his opinion didn't count. So, of all the places to move, why did Mom choose Ridgeport, Long Island? I don't know, probably something like water quality or school SAT scores or the availability of good nursing jobs. I don't think it was because of the magic that's here. That was for me to find out. And I did. I realized that in a town where the stage was reality, I could become a new person.

Of course, I couldn't go too far with this. Mom would have had a heart attack if I'd called myself Ethel or Bernadette or Idina, so I stretched to the limits of my available options. I introduced myself to people as K.C., which isn't exactly a lie, but just as I hoped, they spelled it the way it sounds.

And that's how I became who I am today, Casey.

I became one of those people who need to escape themselves to find themselves. Only I didn't do it via a trip to Oz or Hogwarts or Narnia. I didn't even expect to do it through the Drama Club.

Then I ran into the hurricane known as Brianna Glaser.

Prepare Ye

September 4

1

24 . . . 15 . . . 4.

Casey spun the lock for the third time and pulled on the locker handle. For the third time, nothing happened. She smiled, tried not to look like an idiot, and checked the locker number against the assignment sheet. Yup—217.

The warning bell clanged loud enough to wake a corpse, but no one seemed to notice. Three minutes to homeroom. Later for the locker. She gave the handle one last sharp, futile yank.

Thwack.

The door lurched open, throwing her off balance. It smacked loudly against the locker next to it, causing at least four hundred heads to turn. Casey's backpack slid down her left arm, and as she twisted around in an effort to save it, her belly popped out over her pants, and for some reason she was reminded of yeasty bread rising in a pan. It had not been a great summer for weight, and as she now had a rapt and unwanted audience, she pulled down her shirt, and the pack flung itself onto the floor, sliding across the tiles.

"Fumble!"

A blond boy the size of a Dumpster thumped after the pack, scooping it up. He cradled it briefly, lurching from side to side, faking out no one in particular, then tossed the backpack to another Supersizer, who scrunched it into a roughly oblong shape and lifted it as if to pass.

From behind, a third hulk grabbed the pack roughly and turned toward Casey. Oh, great. Now what? Lessons in Humiliation 101, and her career at Ridgeport wasn't even three minutes old. She thought about the open locker. With a little sucking in, she could squeeze inside, pull the door shut, and stay there the rest of the semester.

Until Hulk Number Three came closer, and she got a good look at him.

"Is this yours?"

He was looming over her now, about nine feet tall. Or maybe six feet three. His shoulders strained the seams of a button-down striped Abercrombie shirt that hung loose over a navy T. Possibly jeans, too, but Casey didn't pick up that detail because she was stuck at the upper half, specifically the eyes, which were blue — well, in the sense that freedom and joy and dancing in a field of wildflowers could be called blue. He cocked his head to the left, causing a shock of sandy-blond hair to fall across his face, which seemed less a motion than a change in the weather, a sudden spring breeze.

He held out the backpack toward her. "Sorry about my friends," he said. "They're animals."

Casey moved her lips, attempting to respond, but no words came out. By the time she could try again he was gone. She watched him bound down the hallway, his head floating above the sea of shorter people.

"Thanks," she squeaked belatedly, to no one.

"Okay, now, breathe."

The voice startled Casey. It belonged to a girl from a locker to her left. She was the type Casey's dad used to call "a tall drink of water."

"Huh?" Casey said.

"He has that effect on everyone," the girl continued. "Girls, guys, teachers. He can't help it. Brianna."

It took Casey a second to realize the girl was naming herself and not the guy.

"Kar— Casey," she replied, pulling back her old name and cringing at the fact that she had to.

"Make up your mind." Brianna laughed, her eyes crinkling into triangles and her mouth showing a little too much gum line, the only flaws in a face that was otherwise all cheekbone framed by blond ringlets. "*His* name, in case you were wondering, and I know you were, is Kyle. Kyle Taggart. Where are you from?"

"Westfield," Casey said, adding as an explanation, "that's in Connecticut."

"Thank you, Carmen Sandiego. Who do you have for homeroom?"

Casey pulled a folded sheet out of her pocket. "Liebowitz."

"Lifer," Brianna said with a nod. "Sometimes forgets things, like his socks or toupee. Two naps short of Alzheimer's. I'm going the same direction."

Casey opened her locker and stashed her jacket and book bag, arranging them so that the jacket hung perfectly, and the bag was available with a quick arm swipe.

"That looks like an ad for a catalog," Brianna observed. "Are you always that neat?"

"Only when I'm nervous," Casey admitted. "It's just first-day jitters."

Brianna grinned and pulled open her own her locker. The inner door was already decorated with family snapshots and magazine photos. A couple of the usual movie stars—Casey was not into them—but also some other shots that she did not expect to see.

"The loves of my life," Brianna said, noticing Casey's curious glance. "The child holding the disgustingly obese hamster is Colter Glaser, my adorably obese brother—"

"Putnam County Spelling Bee . . ." Casey said, glancing at a photo of a white-shirted Latino guy dressed as a kid standing in front of other young men and women, also dressed as kids. She'd seen the show three times, as well as all the other shows represented on Brianna's door.

Avenue Q. Phantom. Les Miz. Wicked . . .

"Jose Llana is so hot, but you could never tell by this picture," Brianna said.

"I know," Casey replied. "I saw him in *Rent*."

Brianna's face brightened. "Me, too. Didn't you just want to jump his bones?"

"Well, I was little, but— "

"Jose, don't take this the wrong way, but we *love* you!" Brianna gave the photo a kiss, shut the locker door, then slid over to Casey's and closed hers. "The trick is, after you do the combination, lift the handle first and *then* pull. If you try to do both together, it sticks. I think Mr. Liebowitz installed these, just after the Depression. Try it and let's go."

Casey did, it worked, and she ran to catch up to Brianna, who was already gliding down the hallway with long, graceful steps.

"Do you sing?" Brianna asked.

"Not really," Casey said. "I'm more an instrument type. Piano, clarinet. I mean, I like to sing, but I've done only regular plays, not musicals. So I kind of suck."

"Sucking is not a relative act. One either sucks or doesn't. No 'kind of' about it. But I'll be the judge of that. In terms of singing, I mean. In any other sense of the word, that's your business." Brianna tossed her a smile and a wink. A *wink*! Casey had never met anyone who actually *winked* in normal conversation. "Now, speaking of sucky singing . . ." Brianna nodded toward a thin girl in fashionably baggy clothes and a fedora, whose red hair flowed nearly to her waist. "That's Darci. You know what we say about Darci. Dances like a butterfly, sings like a bee. Hey, Darse—this is Casey—you coming to the audition?"

"Heeeey!" Darci ran to Brianna and gave her a huge hug, waving to Casey at the same time. "When is it?"

"A week from today, September 11. And if you can sing in tune, which is a big if, callbacks are Thursday."

"LAAAAH!" Darci hooted in a mock operatic voice that sounded, well, pretty sucky.

"Work on it," Brianna said. "A lot." Walking on, she leaned into Casey. "Hope you don't mind. I'm recruiting. Usually, I'm the star, but for this show I'm student director. It's something I've wanted to try, but you can't do that *and* act. Unfortunately."

Casey trailed her around the corner, where a group of guys (and one Goth girl) was playing Magic cards in the hallway. "The two handsome guys," Brianna said, "are Ethan Smith and Corbin Smythe, who sing in the a cappella group, the Vanderdonks, which comes from when this place was the Adriaen Van der Donck School for Boys, I kid you not. Anyway, they have a stand-up act called—three guesses—Smith and Smythe. They are actually funny. The guy in blue is Jason. He can sing, but he acts with his shoulders. Ask him to be happy, he shrugs. Sad, he shrugs. The girl is Lilith. She likes Jason's shoulders very much. Often you will see her crying on them. Hey, guys!"

"Yo!" some of the boys shouted, including Jason, who shrugged.

"Now, Lori Terrell over there, the one with the huge crucifix hanging from her neck, will be singing at the Met someday—that's the Metropolitan Opera, not the museum," Brianna said, waving to a modestly dressed, raven-haired girl who looked like she knew her way around the plus-size rack at Talbot's. "She's a senior. Standing stalwartly beside her is Royce Reardon, also a senior. We call him Royce of No Voice, but he's tried out for every show and he's sweet. And there's Reese, our star dancer-slut, who at the moment is involved in her favorite activity, baring flesh before the clamoring multitudes."

"Hey, Bri," called Reese, a girl with pulled-back red hair who, right there in the hallway, was doing a split that revealed the longest, most perfectly bronzed legs Casey had ever seen—although they were a little hard to see through the thicket of boys surrounding her.

"Drool alert, Mr. Ippolito—all over the floor next to Reese!" Brianna said to a custodian who was approaching with a mop. "Mr. Ippolito, by the way, played Hector, the third Iowan from the right, in this school's 1972 production of *Music Man*."

"How do you know that?" Casey asked.

"I have a photographic memory."

Mr. Ippolito, a gangly man with sandy hair turning silver, began dancing with his mop. "Dancinnnng in the daaaark," he sang. "Do I get a callback?"

"We love you, but keep your day job," Brianna replied.

Casey stared at Brianna in wonder. "How do you do that?"

"Do what?" Brianna said.

"When you say those things about them—do they mind it?"

"They love it," Brianna replied. "That's because it's said with love and honesty. Well, honesty at least. When you *don't* say things, when you pretend or keep secrets—that's when people freak. No secrets, no twisted knickers. That's the motto of the DC. Well, it's not, but it should be."

"The who?"

"DC? You know, *Drama Club*?" Brianna looked at

Casey as if she were scolding a child for forgetting her alphabet. "Which you're about to join?"

"I am?" Casey asked.

"Great! I knew you'd say yes!"

And like that, she was around the next corner.

Back in Westfield, when she was a sophomore, Casey knew a senior who liked to drive close behind trucks, claiming they created pockets of airspace that sucked you along. It was kind of dangerous, he admitted, but it felt great, like you were pulled into a magnetic field. That's what it was like with Brianna. Walking with her in a crowded hallway was like flying on someone else's power. The movement all around them changed—body language, eyes, crowd patterns, everything adjusted to Brianna. She was the only one traveling in a straight line—aside from Casey, who was only borrowing the pocket of airspace.

Casey's Westfield friends had been quiet and studious. The student government and yearbook types. They would have had plenty to say about someone like Brianna, none of it very nice. But Brianna turned expectations upside down.

Brianna stopped in front of Room 147. "Here we are, the Lair of Liebowitz. You know about theater in this school?"

Casey nodded. "The town rolls up on opening night," she said. "Everyone shows up to the musicals. It's like football teams in Texas. The costume and set budgets are six figures—"

"You read about us in the *New York Times*."

"Sunday Arts and Leisure section—"

"Good Lord, you are a total freak." Brianna smiled, and

the sun seemed to blast in through the windowless walls and ceiling. "Like it or not, girl, you are one of us. Have an up-tempo and a ballad prepared for next Tuesday. Ms. Gunderson will accompany, and she can play anything. For callbacks, we'll have sides available. This is not—I repeat, *not*—the Big One. The stores will not shut early, or any of that crap. It's our small fall musical, something new this year—Harrison's idea. He worked on getting permission all summer long. You'll like Harrison; he's Greek, but don't hold it against him. Actually, he's pretty hot, if you like the dark, smoldering, serious type. He swears his eyes are brown, but look closely, they're *black*. Anyway, the show is *Godspell*. Great music. As you know, it's about Jesus, but you don't have to be Christian. Stephen Schwartz wrote it, and he's Jewish. Actually, so was Jesus. You can sing from the show if you want."

"Sides?" Casey said.

"Sections of the script you can read. Scenes. One of the other Drama Club members will read the other characters."

"Okay," Casey said, already numb from trying to remember the details.

"I'm the student director, which means I won't be playing a role. Mr. Levin—he's our faculty adviser—is the actual director, but only because the administration says kids can't direct. Which means I'll mostly be in charge." Brianna looked at her watch. "Gotta go. Hey, do you know Alex Duboff? From Westfield?"

Clang. The sound of the name smacked Casey right back into reality.

"No," she replied. Which was true. Alex had been a classmate, but she didn't *know* him, just knew of him. And she did not feel like expanding this conversation. Looking backward was not in the plan. Who'd have thought Brianna would know Alex Duboff?

"Oh well, just wondering." Brianna shrugged. "Someone I met at the beach over the summer."

"How did you know I lived in Westfield?" Casey asked.

"Uh, because you told me?" Brianna gave her a grave look. "Already the nearness to Liebowitz is corrupting your memory. See you after school."

As she turned to head down the hallway, the bell rang. Immediately kids scrambled toward classes, screaming and giggling. But Brianna did not vary her pace one bit.

"Please have a . . . a . . . seat," came a thick, ragged voice behind her.

Mr. Liebowitz was a craggy old man with a robust salt-and-pepper toupee and a plaid shirt so often washed that you couldn't tell the colors. He smiled warmly at Casey, looking through crooked glasses, then leaned over his attendance sheet. "And you, my dear? You are . . . ?"

Casey quickly rushed over to his desk. "Casey. Casey Chang. There's a mistake on the attendance sheets. May I?"

Before Mr. Liebowitz could answer, Casey took a pen from the desk, crossed out the name "Kara," and wrote in her new name, an action she would repeat eight more times that day.

2

From: <dramakween312@rport.li.com>
To: <rkolodzny@yaleuniversity.edu>
Subject: u wanna change ur last name to sterling???
September 4, 11:07 P.M.

hey, rachel,

y r u never online? dont people im at yale?

ok, about changing ur name. uh, no. rachel KOLODZNY will forever be known as the greatest stage manager of all time at rhs and we are ALL expecting to see that name on bway, so the answer is NO!! get some yalie genius to clone you, call THAT one rachel sterling, and send her back to the drama club cuz we STILL don't have a stage manager (legendary SM shoes are hard to fill!). god we miss you. i miss you. ☹

the fall musical is gonna be godspell. harrison's choice. no, im not gonna be the star of this one. i followed yr recommendation & told mr levin I want to be studnt director. i didn't tell him "cause rachel sez it will look good on my transcript to yale" but i believe it. and besides i am a natural at bossing people around ☺ oh god I will miss acting, tho . . .

oh. there's a new girl in town, casey. sweet and fun. nearly peed when she saw kyle. loves bway shows & knows them all—hosanna and halleluya (sp?)!!! she'd be perfect for the peggy role. description in the cast list: "the shy one. sometimes a little slow to get things, but when she does, she commits all the way." she's perfect for harrison too, but mr. perfect measures both IQs and waistlines with his eyes and in this case both of them are too high for his taste so he will once again miss out on a golden opportunity, but after trying to knock sense into that greek head since we were five years old, i give up.

vre harrison . . .

i love that word—"vre." it's greek for "you asshole," but in a nice way. that's what harrison sez. when his mom & dad say "vre" before your name it means they're annoyed. if you say it right, rrrrolling the r, it's like a slap. an entire culture of people who use asshole as a term of endearment, leave it to the greeks.

i got mad at colter tonight for letting his hamster

loose & called him vre colter. he punched me and i have an unsightly bruise. thinking of suing.

but i digress. i hope casey can act. she says she's done straight plays but you should have seen her lie about knowing this kid from her hometown, alex duboff. bad faking. well, i don't blame her for lying. no one in her right mind would admit knowing that creep.

luv and xoxoxoxox,
bri

"Um, when you say we have three minutes—does that mean *per song* or *per audition?*" asked Lynnette Freeman, whose hair had been cut, streaked, and shaped into something that resembled a sleeping raccoon. Not exactly the style of the musical *Godspell*, but interesting.

"Per audition," Harrison replied for what seemed the hundredth time, holding a sign-up sheet toward her. "We will probably only be hearing *one* of the songs you prepared—but if we need to hear the other, we will ask you. Fill in a slot and give your music to Ms. Gunderson. She'll be playing piano."

Lynnette leaned over to sign the sheet. Behind her was a long line, freshmen to seniors, forty-three by Harrison's count, all waiting to try out for ten roles. Everyone was dressed-up, made-up, buffed-up, hair-styled, nails-colored for the occasion.

Harrison glanced over their heads, looking for Brianna. By now, Brianna should be here. This was not like her. Brianna was usually the first one. She was supposed to have brought the instruction sheets, along with a student helper for sign-up. As the Drama Club vice president, and assistant director of the show, she *should* have been there.

As the club president, Harrison was pissed.

"That's whack, yo," muttered a heavyset guy with a swooping emo haircut. "What if you *do* want to hear two songs? How can we sing a ballad and an up-tempo in three minutes?"

"We'll cut you off," Harrison said. "And you *don't* have to start at the beginning of the song. Just pick the best eight to sixteen bars, show them to Ms. Gunderson, and go from there."

"Bars?" asked Rose Wentworth, a sophomore, peeking over his shoulder.

"Ms. Gunderson goes to bars?" someone else asked. There's always a comedian.

"Bars," Harrison repeated. "Measures. The music between the vertical lines on the page of sheet music."

"We're supposed to have sheet music?"

It was relentless. And it happened every time. You'd think that at a school like Ridgeport, where half these kids could probably be comfortable on a professional stage, they would *know* this stuff. Instead of needing to whine, whine, whine:

"No one ever told us that!"

"Can't we just, like, sing?"

"Can we rap?"

"There's no rap in *Godspell*, dork! Wait. Is there?"

"Do we have to listen to each other's auditions?"

"I have to be out of here by four-fifteen for a cello lesson!"

One . . . two . . . three . . . Harrison counted to calm himself down. "No rapping. You won't listen to each other—you wait in the hall. And no problem, you can sing a cappella." Noticing a few blank responses, he added, "That means without sheet music, without accompaniment. All by yourself."

He felt a firm pinch on his butt, and then Reese draped her arms around him from behind. "Did anyone ever tell you you're hot when you're angry?" she whispered.

"I'm. Not. Angry." Which was true. He was not angry at that moment. He was other things, like frustrated. And . . . something else. Something that always came over him when Reese pulled stuff like this in public. Because Reese, in fact, *was* hot, especially when she put her hands on his chest from behind and breathed in his ear, forcing Harrison out of fear of embarrassment to discreetly place the sign-up clipboard in front of his pants.

"Could have fooled me," she whispered, her breath sweet-scented and warm. He cringed as she ran her fingers through his hair, which was way too thick and never returned to its shape if you messed it up and probably now looked like a brown haystack. "You know, these are normal questions, Harrison. Not everyone is a genius like you. Now calm those fiery black eyes and be cool. You never know where it may lead."

She gave his butt a quick pat (to a chorus of dorky "Oooooh"s from the crowd), then slunk up the aisle to an empty spot in the carpeted row between the orchestra and mezzanine seats. There, as if nothing had just happened, she began to stretch.

"They're not black, they're *brown*," Harrison muttered,

matting his hair back into shape and trying not to look like an idiot. He did not let himself look at her. Looking at Reese meant trying to figure out what she *wanted*, and that was too confusing. They had hooked up once during sophomore year. Tame tongues-and-braces stuff at a party. Didn't talk about it the rest of the year. But Reese had lost the braces and gained oh-so-much-more, and she seemed to want to make up for lost time.

For show, for real—with Reese these days, who knew? And who had time to think about it when the auditorium was in chaos—dancing and singing in the aisles, push-ups and jumping jacks, loud conversations. Darci, her face twisted into either ecstasy or pain, was yodeling (or something) into a distant corner, right next to Ethan Smith and Corbin Smythe from the a cappella group, who were singing a duet, while Lori the opera singer kept repeating "Bbbbbrrrrrrreeeeeee!" in a high-pitched voice, sounding like a sparrow on speed.

Taming the masses was Brianna's job. She was good at it.

Beep. A voice message on his cell phone. Harrison quickly glanced at the screen, which showed the familiar cell number of his dad. Gus Michaels, otherwise known as Kostas Michalakis—patriarch of the Michaels family; renowned proprietor of Kostas Korner: A Gathering Place for Fine Dining at Cheap Prices—who probably wanted Harrison to come and work after school, which meant he'd conveniently forgotten about these auditions despite the fact that Harrison had reminded him at least twenty times. Which made Harrison wonder yet again when his dad was going to realize that there was actually life beyond the diner.

But later for that. He flipped the phone shut.

"Where is the diva?" asked Charles Scopetta, the Drama Club's production designer. Charles had emerged from backstage, cradling a huge papier-mâché sun that covered all but his red Converse sneakers and his eyes, which were peeking out from under an obedient swoop of brown hair that somehow never managed to fall into his eyes. "I need her opinion."

"It looks great," Harrison said.

Charles put the sun down in the aisle and straightened up, ever-so-subtly sucking in his gut to hide what he fondly called the "Final Five," as in pounds-to-lose. "Thank you, but La Glaser has final approval. Not that I don't trust your exquisite taste."

"She's not here yet," Harrison said.

"Oh, I knew it! I *knew* it. Freaking out in the bathroom because she cannot be the star."

"She's the student director. She'll have power."

"Yes, well, she does enjoy that—"

With a sudden *thump* from above, the entire auditorium fell into pitch-blackness. Every conversation, every song, stopped.

"Oops," came a voice from the projection booth. "There seems to be a console problem. Uh, pay no attention to the man in the booth . . . heh-heh . . . "

"Dashiell, damn it, would you please turn on the house lights!" Harrison yelled.

"Temper, temper," Charles said.

"Harrison?" Dashiell shouted as the lights went back on. "Can I show you the source of the problem?

It appears that we have kind of an interesting dilemma . . . "

"Whatever!" Harrison called back. "Come down, please, we need to start!"

"It's rather massive," Dashiell said. "But I'll locate the plug. Wait . . . "

"What planet is he on?" Charles murmured.

"At least he's here," Harrison said. "Where's Brianna? She was supposed get someone to do sign-up—*I shouldn't be doing this.*"

"I know," Charles replied, "you're supposed to be running the launch meeting."

Launch meetings were a Ridgeport tradition– brief, intense, closed-door—where the Drama Club officers recited a Pledge of Conduct before the first audition of every show. It was all about treating auditioners with positive feedback and courtesy. Corny, but it helped. Harrison knew how wound up and emotional these kids felt. He'd been there. In Ridgeport, you started training early—for voice, tap, jazz, ballet, step dancing—and each teacher had a waiting list. (So did the town's shrinks, who did a big business after each round of rejections.) A role meant you were somebody. Your picture, clipped from the newspaper, appeared in the window of every storefront. A total nobody could suddenly move onto the A-list.

"Can one of your people help with the sign-up?" Harrison asked. "I'll get Dashiell and Reese—"

"I'll get Mr. Levin away from Ms. Gunderson," Charles said. "He can help. That's why they pay him the big bucks."

Clutching his papier-mâché sun, Charles jogged down the aisle toward the stage. There, looking as if he were pinned between the Steinway grand piano and the stage, was the faculty adviser, Mr. Greg Levin. The sides of his beard were lifted by a pained smile. Leaning across the piano toward him, her left leg lifted up behind her so her penny loafer dangled from her bare foot, was the French teacher, Ms. Gunderson. She was pert, blond, and had a kind of preppy agelessness. She was also the accompanist for every musical audition—at least every audition since Mr. Levin had become faculty adviser.

"Invite me to the wedding, kids!" Charles called out. "But before that, we have a show to cast?"

"Oh—yes, sorry," Mr. Levin said, his face turning red as he quickly strode up the aisle and put on his plummiest Shakespeare accent: "Once more into the breach!" Mr. Levin was a former actor with an awesome résumé. On Broadway he'd played a man who died a quick, tragic death, in a show that unfortunately did the same thing. He'd starred in an Off-Broadway musical about a talking SUV and had carried a spear dashingly in a Central Park production of *Richard III* with Kevin Kline. He was sharp, funny, smart, could play comedy and drama, and was the greatest living theater FAQ source Harrison ever knew. Whether or not he had a weakness for Ms. Gunderson was hard to tell.

"Are we all here?" he asked Charles.

"The Duchess Brianna will be delayed tonight," Charles replied.

"Oh?" Mr. Levin said. "Is it the SAT prep course, the Intel scholarship meeting, yearbook committee, or Honor Society?"

"Overachievers Anonymous," Charles said.

Mr. Levin smiled. "Ah well, I expect she will appear in the fullness of time." Reaching the back of the auditorium, he took Harrison's clipboard and switched to his booming Voice of the Director: "FRIENDS, ROMANS, AND THESPIANS, AFTER SIGNING UP FOR YOUR SLOT, YOU WILL PROCEED INTO THE HALLWAY AND MAKE YOURSELVES AS COMFORTABLE AS THE CIRCUMSTANCES ALLOW. I WILL CALL YOUR NUMBER AND THE NUMBER OF THE PERSON AFTER YOU, WHO WILL BE 'ON DECK,' AS IT WERE. . . . "

Harrison stepped into the aisle, took Reese by the arm, and called to Dashiell in the booth. "Dashiell. Launch meeting. Backstage. Now."

"Take me away, take me far, far away, out of here . . . " Reese purred.

Harrison paused. "*West Side Story?*"

"Very good. Two points. Three gets you the door prize."

Harrison didn't even want to ask. With Reese trailing him, he ran down the aisle, mounted the steps at stage left, and ran backstage.

He didn't get very far. The wing space at backstage left, normally a bleak, charmless place with cement floors and dust-darkened banks of pulleys, was now a landscape of taffeta poofs, lumpy woolens, old lamps and telephones, rickety tables, hollowed-out bookcases, two-dimensional cars, and fur coats. A group of quiet underclassmen was sifting through the piles, examining material, ripping a seam here and there, bringing more stuff from a room in a distant hallway.

Harrison blurted, "What the f—"

"Watch your language in front of the Charlettes," Charles interrupted. "We're like a family back here."

"A dysfunctional family," Reese said.

"Darling," Charles replied, "dysfunctional or not, the Charlettes are the power behind the stage. The costumes, the scenery, the makeup, the props. Now, due to circumstances beyond our control, there was a flood in the prop room. An act of God. Ha! That fits the play, doesn't it? *Godspell*. Coincidence? Your call."

Vijay Rajput, the tallest and oldest Charlette at six feet three inches and eighteen, dumped a white wig on a pile of costumes. "What mishegas," he said.

"Which means . . . ?" Reese asked.

"Craziness," Vijay said, shaking his head.

Reese gave her best sensitive-girl smile. "I *love* learning Indian words."

"It's Yiddish," Vijay told her.

"Who's going to clean this up?" Harrison demanded.

"That job," said Charles with exasperation, "belongs to the stage manager."

"*We don't have a stage manager!*" Harrison said.

"And whose fault is *that*, Mr. President?" Charles asked.

Harrison stewed. It was a good question. The fall show had been his idea, but it was already September, and neither he nor Brianna had had the time to look for a good SM. Last year's SM, Rachel Kolodzny, had done the job for four years with style, but she was now at Yale, and no one else had been trained. And Harrison's younger cousin Stavros, who was dying to do the job, had moved to Brooklyn over the summer and was a freshman at a city high school. "We just can't leave everything a mess, Charles. We have to do some of the work ourselves."

"You don't mean the officers?" Reese asked, sounding alarmed.

"Certainly not," Charles assured her. "The president, VP, designer, tech guru, and choreographer—we are *creative royalty*. We do *not* clean up."

"Charles . . ." Harrison said warningly.

"Well, okay, maybe a tiny bit."

"Let's begin the launch meeting," Harrison said. "Where's Dashiell?"

Harrison stepped back, pulled aside the curtain, and looked out into the house. Students were still clustered near the sign-up desk, talking to Mr. Levin. Beyond them, way in the back, a large black-metal box with legs wobbled down the aisle.

It was Dashiell, carrying a huge soundboard that covered him from waist to head. He picked up speed as he approached the side doors.

The doors were in an alcove. One of them flew open, and a harried-looking Asian girl rushed in. Her face was furrowed with worry, her eyes fixed on the crowd of auditioners. From her vantage point, she could not see Dashiell barreling toward her.

"Hey, you at the door!" Harrison shouted, waving his hands frantically. *"Heads up!"*

The girl looked at him.

And Dashiell, oblivious to it all, plowed right into her.

With a sickening crash, the machine, Dashiell, and the new girl collapsed to the floor.

3

CASEY GASPED FOR BREATH. ABOVE HER, THE faces blurred in and out—and voices, a thrum of sound. Beyond them she saw the fractured edges of a metallic shape that was once intact. The scene began to fade, and in her mind she was somewhere else . . .

A quiet spring day, rising from the sidewalk, floating through a sea of people, catching a glimpse of another metallic shape . . .

No!

She sat up quickly with a gasp, forcing herself to focus.

The faces coalesced. These were Ridgeport High School students. It was audition night, in the Murray Klein Memorial Auditorium.

A very tall, very skinny guy with chocolate skin and narrow glasses stood bent in shock, his hands flat to the side in a classic Macaulay Culkin pose. "You were in my trajectory . . . I—I created this blind spot . . . It wasn't intentional . . . oh my God . . . "

He had hit her. A few feet away, a large black electronic unit with lots of dials lay diagonally against the aisle seats. It was huge and expensive-looking, not crushed but definitely broken. "Ouch. Sorry. Did I break your computer?" Casey asked.

"It's . . . a console. Analog. Technically not a computer. As for its brokenness, well, that's complicated. We were about to examine it for defects . . . "

A smaller group led by a bearded, dark-eyed teacher and fretful-looking blond-haired woman, barged through the circle of students that surrounded Casey. The man spoke first. "I'm Greg Levin, the faculty adviser. Are you all right?"

"I'm fine, thanks," Casey replied.

"Dashiell, you nearly killed her," Harrison said.

"*You* instructed me in no uncertain terms to bring the console down!" Dashiell protested.

"I *meant*—"

"Guys, let's give some help to . . . ?" Mr. Levin offered Casey his arm.

"Casey," she replied.

All three guys reached down to help her, and Mr. Levin began making introductions. "This is Harrison, president of the Drama Club; Charles, our costume and set designer; and Dashiell, our tech guy, who does lighting and sound.

And right behind them, that's Reese, our choreographer, and Ms. Gunderson, our accompanist."

Casey stood, breathing steadily now. She was winded and bruised, but it could have been worse. As the crowd backed off, people started to clap. Casey forced a smile, but the attention was *not* what she'd had in mind.

At the moment, going home seemed like a very good idea. A few minutes earlier she *had* been headed home. She'd chickened out, not wanting to subject the public to the same torture she'd faced all week practicing in front of a mirror. What brought her back to school was guilt. She had promised Brianna she would show up. And now that she had destroyed a machine and made a fool of herself in the grand Kara Chang Tradition of Being in the Utterly Wrong Place at the Utterly Wrong Time because of her desire to please Brianna Glaser, where *was* Brianna?

Not here. Which meant Casey didn't have to be here either. "Okay, well, I guess I'm too late to audition," she said, edging toward the door.

"Audition?" said Dashiell.

"You still want to audition after that?" Charles asked.

"No problem," said Harrison. "We'll add a slot."

"But—but—" Casey stammered.

"Did you all hear that?" Mr. Levin said, turning to the crowd. "This young woman's attitude, ladies and gentlemen, is called *heart! Three cheers for Casey!*"

More applause. Casey cringed. Everyone had totally misunderstood her.

Harrison held out the sign-up sheet, which had an empty line drawn across the bottom. Which meant not only did she have to stay, but she would be here until dinnertime. Swallowing hard, she signed her name and sank into an aisle seat. Mr. Levin, Ms. Gunderson, Harrison, Dashiell, and the other Drama Club members assembled by the edge of the stage.

"Okay, now that our adventure is over, let's start!" Mr. Levin announced. "To those of you who are new to the school, or to the audition process, this show is a bit different from our big spring production. The spring musical is about bigness, polish, and pizzazz, but the fall show is something new and exciting. A way to remind ourselves *why* we're in the theater. A small, intimate cast, only ten people. We'll really dig into the roles, experiment a little, without the pressure of massive crowd scenes and dances. There will be lots of creative input from students, from lead roles to directing to props. The score will be played by a small rock band."

"And don't forget," piped up one of the Drama Club officers, "even if your audition really sucks, there may be a bright future for you backstage in theater design with the award-winning Charlettes!"

"Thank you, Charles," Mr. Levin said. "Now, remember, this is not *American Idol* and we have no Simon Cowell—"

"*Hold the presses!*" a familiar voice shouted from the back.

Mr. Levin looked toward the doorway, where Brianna was tromping in with a group of very large guys. "Sorry, sorry, sorry," she called out, "I was convincing my boys to come, and they're tough customers. Did I miss the launch meeting?"

"We didn't have it," Harrison said from the stage. "There wasn't enough time."

"Uh-oh, that's bad luck," Brianna said, walking straight up to Harrison. "But I'll make up for it. The sign-up sheet, please."

"Sorry, we're all filled up," Harrison snapped. "And you *know* you're not allowed to take a role."

"It's not for me," Brianna said.

"Add more slots, Harrison," Reese suggested. "You did it for Casey."

Brianna snatched the clipboard from Harrison's hand. Immediately the guys behind her started hooting and shouting:

"Boo-yah! Boo-yah!"

"Where's the karaoke mike?"

"Mi-mi-mi-miiii! Hey, can I try out first?"

Harrison's jaw went slack in disbelief. Reese was cracking up. Charles had his head in his hands. Ms. Gunderson's smile had frozen tight. And Mr. Levin looked like he couldn't decide whether to laugh or throw them all out.

Casey's nervousness suddenly subsided. The pain in her side, too. Mainly because one of the guys was Kyle. Her eyes followed him as he headed for the hallway, surrounded by the jumping, hand-pumping throng of football guys.

"What the hell was *that* all about?" Harrison asked.

Brianna smiled. "This will be *so* worth it, guys. You'll see."

"It better be," Harrison grumbled.

Casey, for one, didn't mind a bit. All the auditioners would have to wait in the hall. And as long as Kyle was there, the view would be just fine.

4

"COME WITH ME."

Casey wasn't expecting to be pulled by the hand like a child. But she couldn't do much but follow as Brianna yanked her up the sloping aisle, across the row that divided the front and back sections, not stopping until they'd nestled into the last row of the auditorium, hidden in the shadows.

"God, is he pissed at me," Brianna said.

"Who?" Casey asked, nervously eyeing the door through which the other auditioners were obediently filing.

"Dark Eyes. Harrison. Okay, I was late. I am usually all about being on time, but I had a reason. A good one. Unfortunately, Harrison hates it when things aren't just exactly right. He's a control freak. And no one ever tells him off, because he's not only Mr. Smart, Talented, Perfect, but also Most Likely to Win a Tony for Best Actor."

The door to the lobby thumped shut. The auditioners had left except for Royce, who was pacing on the stage. Harrison, Ms. Gunderson, and Mr. Levin huddled around the piano. Dashiell, Reese, and Charles were sitting in the seats, chatting, waiting.

Only the Drama Club officers were supposed to be watching the auditions, Casey realized. "Shouldn't I be outside . . .?" she began.

"Brianna?" Harrison called over his shoulder. "Are you joining us?"

"Just listening from the back to hear how the singers project!" Brianna called back, pulling from her backpack a clipboard with a stack of preprinted evaluation sheets. She lowered her voice. "I hope you don't mind, Casey. I mean, you're fine sitting here with me. I'm nervous. I have to talk to you. I had a religious experience last night. It was like Michelangelo seeing the soul in the human form. Or Einstein seeing . . . whatever . . . the relative in relativity."

Mr. Levin called out from the stage: "Royce? Singing 'Some Enchanted Evening' from *South Pacific*? We're ready for you. So sorry for the delay. *Take it away, Royce!*"

Brianna sighed. " Introducing Royce of No Voice."

"'Some enCHANTed eeeeveniiiiiiing . . . '" Royce's singing sounded like a cross between a car horn and a blown nose.

"Please, Casey," Brianna said, "do not judge Royce by his audition. In real life, we adore him. And he tries so hard . . . "

On the evaluation sheet Brianna quickly wrote Royce's name and then, in the space allotted for Musicianship, Presence, Dramatic Movement, etc., drew a quick sketch:

Casey swallowed hard. She wondered what Brianna did to people she *didn't* adore.

"Okay, so the other night I went to a party at Scott Borland's," Brianna said, tucking her toilet into her stack of papers. "This is something I never do because Scott and his friends are proof of evolution, being clearly descended from baboons. But his house is awesome in a stupid-rich way, so worth the trip sociologically. Anyway, after about forty minutes Scott reveals this karaoke setup. He starts to sing, totally drunk, and before things can get uglier, I'm out of there. But as I run through the house, suddenly I hear the same song—only it's amazing. Like Justin Timberlake sexy. Someone in the den, playing video games, singing along with Scott, thinking no one is listening. So I sneak closer, just outside the door, and I peek in . . . "

"'Then fly to her siiiide . . . and make her your oooOOORK!'" Royce's voice cracked painfully.

"Thanks, Royce, that was great," Mr. Levin said. "Callbacks will be posted tomorrow. On your way out, can you ask Kathy Marshall to come in?"

Brianna wrote Kathy's name on the evaluation sheet. "Of course he stops when he sees me. He blushes and says he only sings in the shower—which, come to think of it, would be an interesting place to hold his audition—but then, just like that, he stands up, bows, takes my hand, and *dances with me* . . . while singing 'On the Street Where You Live.' From *My Fair Lady*? How does he even *know* that song? He says his mom listens to show tunes. Everyone in his house sings; they don't make a big deal out of it. My heart is thumping. My brain is turning to ramen noodles. But I'm also thinking: Do we actually have a leading man for the show?"

"I thought you said Harrison was a future Tony winner," Casey said.

Suddenly Kathy Marshall's voice called out from the stage: "My song will be 'I Dreamed a Dream' from *Les Misérables*."

"Harrison is an *actor*," Brianna replied. "He can do anything—old men, little kids, bad guys, comic roles, accents. You want a guy like him for the most difficult role, the role no one else can do. For a leading man, you need charm, sex, great shoulders, hair. Eye candy. If you get a voice, too—well, hallelujah!"

"Who is this guy?" Casey asked.

"You'll see." Brianna looked longingly at the stage.

"I can't believe I'm not auditioning," she said, almost under her breath. "You are so lucky. But hey, I made the choice. Sometimes you have to take new paths. Colleges like that."

Kathy's singing voice was every bit as sweet as Royce's was terrible. It was the kind of voice that reached out and caressed you. Casey was disappointed when she was stopped in the middle of the song.

Next to her, Brianna was already busy writing:

Voice 6, Looks 5, Acting 4.
Not bad. Not great. Forgettable.

"I thought she was good," Casey said.

"You haven't been to a Ridgeport audition before," Brianna replied.

The next auditioner, Lori, sang a religious song that bounced off the walls, filling the auditorium. Then, while everyone just stared in awe, she sang a few bars of some Italian opera song.

Voice 9, Looks 7, Acting 5.
Fabulous legit singing. (Too bad Godspell is not an opera.)
Call back.

Next was Corbin Smythe, who cracked everybody up with Gaston's song from *Beauty and the Beast* and went on to sing an incredibly sweet "Loch Lomond" in a Scottish accent.

Decent comedic skills.
Okay voice.
Possible keep.

Casey swallowed hard. She had always thought of herself as picky, but not like this.

"Casey? . . . Casey Chang?"

It took a moment for Casey to realize that Harrison was calling her name.

"That's you, girl," Brianna reminded her.

"Can't be," Casey said. "I signed up way at the bottom."

"Damn, forgot to tell you." Brianna slapped her forehead. "I saw your name all the way down there when Harrison gave me the sheet. There was a cross-out near the top, so I moved you up. I just figured you'd get it over earlier. That was okay, no?"

"No!" Casey cried out.

"Casey?" Harrison called out. "Is that you?"

"Yes," Casey squeaked. She rose from her seat on shaky legs. She felt like she wanted to throw up.

"Hey, want me to ask Harrison to change the slot?" Brianna offered.

Casey almost said yes, until she realized it would mean experiencing this awful feeling twice. Best to get it over with now. "It's . . . okay," she said.

Brianna smiled and hugged her. "You go, girl. 'You'll be swell . . . you'll be great.' Quick, what musical is that from?"

"I . . . don't have a photographic memory like you," Casey replied numbly, staggering into the aisle.

As she slumped toward the stage, clutching her sheet music, Ms. Gunderson chirped, "What will you be singing for us?"

Casey had to read the song title to remind herself. "'The Colors of the Wind'? From *Pocohantas*?"

Ms. Gunderson immediately began playing it . . . without the music. By heart. She *knew* it already. As Casey wobbled past the piano toward the stage, Ms. Gunderson was getting to the part in the music where Casey was supposed to start singing.

Right . . . now.

Crap. The song had begun, and Casey hadn't even reached the stairs to the stage. What was she supposed to do—sing as she was climbing them? *Get up there—move, any way you can!* her brain screamed.

She lurched to the left and ran for the stairs. Her right foot caught on the bottom step, causing her left foot to thump down loudly on the second step.

"Are you okay?" asked Mr. Levin, rushing toward her. The way he was looking at her was easy to read: This girl is an accident waiting to happen.

"No rush, I'll vamp until you're ready," Ms. Gunderson said cheerfully, playing the introduction over again.

Casey walked out to the center of the stage. She took a deep breath. She had practiced her song at least a hundred times. She had planned every facial expression, every gesture. She remembered what her drama teacher in Westfield had told her: *Don't move your eyebrows so much. Think of your eyes as spotlights, and stand still unless you have a reason to move.*

She glanced into the darkened audience and saw Brianna's shadow in the back, poised with a pencil. Suddenly Ms. Gunderson's notes sounded totally unfamiliar, like some ancient Icelandic folk chant. Casey took a breath, prayed for the right key . . . and squeaked. Loud. She felt as if someone had crawled inside her and sandpapered her throat. "C-can I start again?" she croaked.

"No problem, sweetie," Ms. Gunderson said, vamping some more.

But at the moment she opened her mouth again, a scream rang out from backstage, followed by a loud CRRRRRASHHH!

Charles leaped from his seat in the auditorium. "Charle-e-ettes!" he shouted. "Oh, good Lord, time out." As he jogged onstage, he said to Casey, "Sorry, doll—at Ridgeport, half the drama is backstage. Go ahead. I'll listen from there."

Vamp . . . vamp.

Casey started again. She sang the right words. She moved her eyes and her arms to the music. Sort of. The sound from her mouth seemed tiny and raw. It didn't help to hear the hiss of arguing voices coming from backstage. She couldn't bear to look at anyone, so she stared into the empty seats on the left side of the auditorium. This was torture. Nothing like yearbook. Answering questions, assigning tasks—*that* she could handle. Not this!

About halfway through, Ms. Gunderson started playing really softly, then not at all. Harrison was standing up, looking at her.

Casey's voice tailed off like a dying bird.

"Thank you," Harrison said pointedly, as if he'd said it

several times before. "That was great. Callbacks will be posted tomorrow."

"You're welcome. I mean, thanks."

That was it. The audition was over. One song. A *quarter* of a song.

Casey wanted to take it back. She wanted to rewind time, to before the backstage argument. To before Brianna had changed her sign-up. To before the collision with Dashiell. It wasn't fair. The cards had been stacked against her.

Harrison had called her "great." But that's what he'd said to Royce, too. This must be another Ridgeport tradition. Lying to the Tone-Deaf and Talentless.

Brianna was writing something on her sheet. What was it?

Another toilet? A cesspool? An atomic bomb? There was no way Casey could face her on the way out.

Instead she ran backstage, hoping no one could see her burst into tears.

5

Dr. Fink,
can't make tomorrow's therapy session. the
reason is i have 2b here. pipes burst in
the prop/costume room. chaos. am curbing
perfectionistic tendencies very well but
not sudden rages. am on the verge of
quitting. bet you didn't think you'd hear
me say that. lol. hope you get this txt msg
before the 24-hour cancellation rule!!!
how about Sat. 4 pm?
charles s

Charles snapped shut his cell phone. "Oh, please, people! You act as though I flooded the prop room on purpose, just to make you work!" he hissed at the pouting Charlettes, who were taking things out of the prop/costume room and listlessly dumping them on the backstage floor. This offended every one of the Five Senses of Charles Scopetta: Order, Loyalty, Style, Relentless Dedication, and Fun.

And when any of the Five Senses was violated, Charles was inclined to lash out. Which was a bad habit he had been working on, to the tune of expensive weekly visits with Dr. Eustis Fink the Useless Shrink. So, per Dr. Fink's instructions, he counted to three (internally) and said (calmly), "This is the theater, darlings. We go on. And"—he picked up a wig that had been dumped on the floor and looked like a dead possum—"we do *not* "—he hung up a military uniform that had been thrown over an armchair—"*MAKE A MESS!*"

The Charlettes were staring at him. With their slouches and slack, surly features, they resembled a Calvin Klein ad for the pimple set. Charles forced a smile. Everything seemed suddenly very quiet. It took him a moment to realize that the girl—Casey—had just finished her audition. Oh, lovely. He had barely heard her. He should have been out there with the other DC officers, but no, he had been busy text-messaging his shrink and dealing with the prima donna freshmen and sophomores who thought it was beneath them to clean up. This year's batch of Charlettes needed a training session. Boot camp. A spanking. *Something.*

"My fingers are schmutzy," said Vijay.

"Okay, um, so where are these supposed to go?" said Ruby Dionne, holding two spiked World War I helmets.

"And where do we put these ostrich features?" asked a freshman named Dan Winston.

"Well, let's see . . ." Charles began. "How about up your—"

With a *whoosh*, the backstage curtain opened, mercifully cutting off Charles's answer, and a blur of hair, shirt, and jeans rushed past him.

"Wrong exit, honey," Charles called out. "Try again. With feeling."

"Ggghhh . . ." she replied, her voice strangled by tears, her body blocked by the mound of costumes and props that lay between her and the exit. It was Casey, the girl who had just auditioned. "Sorry," she said, between jerking sobs. "S-sorry!"

Charles bolted up from the chair. She was upset. Damn, he *had* to curb the catty remarks. "No, *I'm* sorry," he said, leading her toward the card table. "I'm a jerk, ask anyone here. Look, I take back what I said. You can use any exit you want, okay? You can use *two* exits—go out that door, come back in, and then use the one near the big room."

Casey smiled a little. "That's . . . not why I'm upset."

"That's a relief. For me. Doesn't do *you* a lot of good. Come and sit. We're having a crisis back here, too. Maybe we can share miseries." Charles gestured to the table, but on each chair was a plastic but nonetheless surprisingly realistic World War I helmet, complete with tasseled spike pointing straight upward. "Ouch. We'll, uh, move them first."

He handed her a handkerchief and swept aside two of

the helmets. As they sat, she wiped her eyes. "Thank you for not laughing," she said.

"Oh?" Charles said. "Is there a reason to laugh? Tell me, I *need* one."

"I meant, at my audition?"

"Please!" Charles said in his best heartily scoffing voice. "You were way better than my first time. Why do you think I'm back here with these losers—because I love to fondle gowns soaked in sweat from 1993? Well, yes, but you should have heard *my* audition. Harrison nearly passed out during my ballad. The school nurse rushed in thinking I was dying of strangulation. So I read the handwriting on the wall. I found my bliss elsewhere."

Casey smiled, her eyes slowly taking in the enormity of the mess. "And . . . this is it?"

"I design. That's what I do. I make things beautiful. This mess is something different. It's what happens when you lose a stage manager, the prop room floods, and your loyal underlings turn against you. Normally, we're very cuddly and milk-and-cookies back here."

Casey smiled. Judging from the little gut that pooched over his belt, Charles had had much happy experience with milk and cookies. Somehow that made her feel at ease.

"Well, there's plenty of space to put things away while the room dries?" Casey said.

"Is that a question or a statement?"

Casey blushed. "Sorry. I do that sometimes when I'm nervous. The uplift. It's a statement? I mean, it's a statement! You can reorganize. You need to reorganize. Okay, I'm telling you. Reorganize."

"Bossy thing, aren't you? I was thinking of a Dumpster. There's one out back, near the construction site for the new wing." Charles grinned. "Which adds to the other two new wings that have been built during our lifetimes, and which, upon completion, will finally allow the school to fly away."

Aha. A laugh. Casey was loosening up. She stood, picking up a few helmets. She eyed the fretwork of pulleys and taut vertical ropes against the wall and stacked the helmets snugly behind some of them. "How about here? By the time you need these ropes to raise and lower the backdrops, the prop room will be dry." She picked up a fistful of empty hangers and hooked them onto a horizontal metal pipe just over her head. "This will hold a lot of weight. You can get the costumes off the floor." She glanced at the Charlettes, who did seem pretty motley. "Um, can you guys give me a hand?"

As she began picking up the garments, Vijay, who had been leaning against the wall, scooped up a jacket or two. "She's cool," he said to Charles.

"I'm about to faint," Charles replied.

The other Charlettes pitched in to help, too. They found old boxes and vases and stuffed them with props. They made shelves out of music stands. They made a discard pile of old useless material.

Charles quietly sneaked away and scurried back into the audience. Back to his Drama Club audition duties.

"Everything okay back there?" Harrison whispered.

Charles nodded. "We are in very good hands."

He sat back and listened—a Kelly Clarkson soundalike, a guy with a sweet high-pitched voice, a girl who speed-sang. Aisha, Jamil, Becky. All good. Charles liked auditions from this side of the stage. His dad used to say the eyes were the windows to the soul, but he was wrong. You could hide things with your eyes. Singing was being naked. Nothing hidden. Whoever you were—timid, brave, tender, tough, unsure, giving, selfish—it all came through when you sang, whether you wanted it to or not.

They were nearing the end of the list when Mr. Levin excused himself for a break.

Harrison was smiling. "This is great. I think we already have what we need."

"Not yet," Brianna said. "Just wait."

"Meaning . . . ?" Harrison said.

"Meaning just wait," Brianna shot back.

Harrison's smile tightened. "You know I hate secrets."

"You know I am all about secrets," Brianna said. "And this is why we adore each other, *vre* Harrison."

Oh, the tension, Charles thought. *Mr. Control and Ms. Over-the-Top.* Being near those two had the same effect as dunking your head in a bowl of Starbucks espresso. But he was distracted by quiet laughter filtering out from backstage. With the Charlettes these days, that was not a good sign. "Excuuuuse me again," Charles said, rolling his eyes. Tucking his clipboard under this arm, he ran onto the stage and slipped behind the curtain.

Near the far wall, around a card table, sat Casey, Vijay, Ruby, and the other Charlettes. The table was stacked neatly with gloves, paper fans, fake phones, and electronic equipment. The floor had been swept clean and the wing space was festooned with costumes and props, everything neatly in place.

Charles's clipboard dropped to the floor. "I'm dreaming," he said.

Casey looked tentative. "Sorry . . . ?"

"Sorry about what? How did you *do* this?"

"It wasn't that hard," Casey said.

"Wasn't that hard?" He lifted her and spun her around, screaming with glee like something out of a cheesy movie, but he didn't care. "Will you marry me?"

"Um . . . " Casey giggled, embarrassed. "I guess . . . if you design the dress."

Vijay bolted out of his chair, looking thoroughly disgusted. "Oy. My stomach."

Ms. Gunderson began playing again. The audition. Charles had almost forgotten about the audition. He forced himself to listen. It was a familiar intro.

When a male voice began to sing, all conversation stopped. Time stopped.

The sound was so clear and sexy and strong and human, it was like the *thing* itself with a shape and a life. It soared and floated. It filled the stage. Charles had heard "On the Street Where You Live" sung a million times, but never like this.

He tiptoed to the curtain. One by one the Charlettes joined him.

"He's a god," said Dan Winston.

"He's a natural," whispered Charles.

Casey put the pieces of the puzzle together. "He's a religious experience."

As the song ended, Kyle smiled into the audience and then began to stroll off the stage. No one moved or made a sound until he got to the stairs.

"Uh, do you have an up-tempo?" Ms. Gunderson squeaked.

Kyle stopped. "An up-what?"

"Never mind." Harrison's voice popped up from the dark auditorium. "Kyle, would you come back tomorrow for callbacks?"

"Tomorrow?" Kyle said. "Aw, damn, I have to go to practice. I can't play because of the ankle, but I'm part of the team and—"

"Cancel it," Brianna told him. "This is mandatory."

As Kyle started toward the auditorium doors, limping but whistling, Brianna could barely stay in her seat. She was right. She had called it. Nailed it when no one else even guessed.

She knew his type.

Some people had it and forced it on people, like Reese. Other people had it but chose to hold back.

Underpromise, overdeliver. That was his MO. Don't let on. Don't let them see you sweat. Nurse your talent in secret. Then, when the others least expect it, blow them all out of the water. Brianna admired that. Kyle was her opposite. For Brianna, all the effort showed. She screamed Type A no matter how hard she tried to hide it. So people expected the 97 average, the SAT score of 2300, the drama-queen performances, and fashionista clothes. Anything less, and they talked. But Kyle—nothing about him was expected. Just when you thought you had him pegged, he proved you wrong. He was a force of nature. A major talent. She'd known it the moment she'd heard him singing at Scott's party that night. That was sexy enough.

But the fact that he didn't need to show off, that he kept it inside until he was good and ready . . .

She couldn't think about this. Because when she did, she couldn't think about anything else. Brianna didn't know many people like Kyle. She wanted to know him. She had to.

She watched him heading for the door, shooting her a thumbs-up, grinning like a three-year-old. Like a kid who just gotten away with something, just played with the coolest toy in the room while no one was watching. And that was when the thought hit her—maybe he just *didn't know.*

Could he not know how talented he was? Was it possible he couldn't tell what an impact he created? God, the air in the room had changed. From now on in the Drama Club, it would be BK and AK: Before Kyle and After Kyle. Brianna knew that in her gut.

As the auditorium door shut, Charles emerged from behind the curtain. "Did I just die and go to heaven?"

Brianna ran down from the mezzanine. Her head was buzzing. Her pores felt wide open, as if she had just taken a long shower. "You're welcome, everybody! Now you know why I was late. He wanted to play catch with his teammates. I had to yank him away."

"He's beautiful." Reese sighed.

"Who knew?" Ms. Gunderson said.

Mr. Levin looked skeptical. "If he were in the show, could he make a commitment? This is football season, and he's the star of the team."

"Not this year," Brianna said. "Over the summer he hurt his ankle in a cribbage—"

"Scrimmage," Harrison corrected her.

"So he's out for the season," she went on. "He was in a cast until last week, in case you didn't notice. Which is why trying to play catch with his buddies was insane, and why I was able to get him to come here."

Dashiell nodded solemnly. "You have an awesome ability to spot talent, Brianna. It's a unique gift. I have always admired that in you—"

"He's perfect for the lead role," Reese interrupted, throwing Harrison a provocative look. "For Jesus."

Harrison gave her his best I-don't-give-a-crap look. Brianna recognized it. Nonchalance was one of his specialties as an actor, even when he was mad jealous, which he had to be right then. If there was one thing Brianna had expertise in, it was Harrison's ego. "I agree. The guy is a natural," he said through slightly gritted teeth.

"Well, let's not cast him yet," Brianna said diplomatically. "He still has to get through callbacks."

"Yes, that's what I meant," Harrison snapped. "I meant callbacks."

"Don't be upset," Brianna said. "I was just trying to recruit good people."

"You did great," Harrison told her with a tight little smile. "One star. One dud. A five hundred average. That's good. Now let's move on."

Charles took in a sudden sharp breath. "You did *not* say that," he whispered, looking over his shoulder.

"What?" Harrison asked.

A door slammed backstage, loudly.

"Damn . . . " Charles said, running onto the stage. Brianna followed close behind him, along with the other DC members.

He pulled aside the curtains. The backstage area was beautiful. Immaculate. The Charlettes were standing around a card table, looking shell-shocked.

Charles ran to the door, opened it, and looked out into the hallway. "She's gone."

"Who?" asked Reese.

"Casey." Charles sank into a chair.

Harrison winced. "No. Did she hear?"

Charles rolled his eyes. "With a voice like yours, Mr. Project-to-the-Back-Row? Of course she heard."

"Yeah, that really sucked," said Vijay softly.

Brianna glanced at the tidy boxes, the neat rows of costumes. "This is beautiful. Who did this?"

"Our beloved dud," Charles said.

From: <harrison.michaels@rport.li.com>
To: <stavrosdagreek@nyc.cable.net>
Subject: sup?
September 11, 6:32 P.M.

Yo, Stavros,

Hey, cuz. Sup in NYC? Stuyvesant High School sounds cool. Dad is still calling your dad O Adelphos Mou o Leventis. My brother the hero. Sixteen years ragging on each other, and now that he opened a restaurant in Brooklyn Heights he's a saint. Now Dad points to the $10.95 pot roast special in the diner and tells everyone his brother can get $24 for the same thing . . . "a la carte!" Hey, are your shows as good as ours? Right. Maybe the kids are smarter. Smarter than me, anyway. I screwed up big time at auditions today. I think I nuked a possible perfect stage manager. You're right, I have a big mouth and I'm a friggin know-it-all. I can tell you that now because I don't have to see your ugly face laughing at me.

Oh, by the way, we're doing Godspell. Can't wait to get my halo. This will look good on my resume.

Later,
Harrison

6

CASEY SLAMMED THE DOOR BEHIND HER. THE living room windows shook, but it didn't matter. No one was home. Her mom was working, and Casey herself didn't count anyway. She was a nobody, a no-talent.

What did she expect—just because she had moved away, just because she had changed her name, things would be different? Somehow she'd magically know how to do things right for a change? She would somehow become another person? She was still the same klutz. A bad-luck magnet by any name.

She stomped upstairs, hoping her heavy footfalls would break through the stairs and she'd go tumbling, tumbling, down into a dark and bottomless rabbit hole like Alice in Wonderland and find a world where everything was turned upside down and inside out. Where the unexpected was expected. The fantasy world she deserved, not the fantasy world of Casey Chang, Normal Girl, which she would never, *ever* see.

The headache had started on the way home, in the back of her head. Running upstairs made her temples throb. She flopped onto her mattress and closed her eyes. The bed frame thumped hollowly against the wood paneling, which had been painted white but still made her new room look like a set from *The Brady Bunch*.

No matter how hard she tried to block it out, the audition ran like a loop in her head. How could everything have gone so wrong? How could her voice have acted like that, like a wounded bird never quite finding its flight path? And then backstage, where she let herself be *used* like that! Cleaning up like Cinderella while they laughed behind her back.

Casey the dud.

They didn't know her. They didn't know what she could do—what she *used* to be able to do back when she was Kara the class officer, the yearbook editor . . . Kara the Unafraid.

She groaned. The train of thoughts made her head hurt even more. And now her cell phone was beeping.

She reached over and pulled it out of her shoulder bag.

hey everything ok? kc harrison didnt mean it. hes ok, really, just talks tough sometimes . . . txt me, ok?

It was from Brianna.

The possible replies ran through Casey's mind: *Leave me alone. I'm pissed at you* (true but harsh). *Thanks* (strong and silent but too cold and mysterious). *No problem, it wasn't your fault, I'm okay* (why not just walk all over me?).

She turned the phone off.

Dropping it back into her bag, she noticed her laptop glowing dully on her desk. She sat up and reached for the mouse, jiggling it so the screen would come to life. Not one IM. Which shouldn't have been surprising, considering that she had deleted her old friends from her buddy list the day she arrived here. At the time it had made sense, a part of her master plan to erase the past, but now the deletion seemed like a colossally dumb idea. It would be nice to talk to someone old and familiar. There was only one thing from her past she hadn't let go of.

Tentatively she opened a desk drawer. Reaching under a pile of papers, she pulled out a frayed envelope. Her hands shook as she removed a photograph from inside. It was thin and yellowing, cut from a newspaper, and it showed a young, handsome dad and two adorable, smiling kids—a blond, floppy-haired, gap-toothed boy of about seven and a shy-looking girl maybe two years younger. Beneath the photo was a caption that began "Kirk Hammond and Family."

As tears filled Casey's eyes, the photo went blurry. She wondered what would happen if she just disappeared, just wandered into the ocean with rocks in her pocket, or flung herself from the Empire State Building. Would anyone care?

Her mom would. Really, that was the only reason Casey

kept herself from doing anything stupid. Mom cared.

She tucked the photo into the envelope and shoved it back in the drawer. Falling onto her bed, she began to sob quietly, closing her eyes. No matter how hard you tried, some things never went away. The thought led her into a dream, a dream that was a scattered collage of the day . . . the collision with Dashiell, the awful audition, the tidying up backstage, the insult . . . dud . . .

Dud-dud-da-DUD-dud-dud . . .

She was hearing music now, a rhythm. It filtered into her brain and became words, lyrics to a familiar song. "Day by Day," from *Godspell*.

Casey's eyes blinked open.

The song wafted in through her window, from outside. The voices were too clear, too raw-sounding to be a recording—soft voices without instruments, a cappella. Real voices. Coming nearer. Breaking into harmony. Clapping rhythmically. A gospel solo broke out over the chorus.

"What the—?" She sat up and wiped her face with a tissue. Trudging to the window, she flung it open.

The view was so incongruous, she thought she was in one of those strange states in which you were half awake but still smack in the middle of some whacked-out dream. Below her, dancing on her lawn, were Brianna, Harrison, Dashiell, Charles, and Reese. Dashiell was singing the solo. She knew why he was a tech guy. They all smiled up at her, raising their arms. They looked like a rescue squad, a curiously happy and welcoming rescue squad beckoning her to jump.

"We're so sorry, Casey Chang . . ." sang Dashiell to the tune.

Casey scraped her fingernail on the windowpane. It hurt. That meant this was real. Didn't it?

Harrison, like a fussy orchestra conductor, waved his arms, stopped everyone from singing, and counted off: "One, two, ready, go!"

"For she's a jolly good fellow, okay, not really a fellow, but we can't rhyme too well, oh! Do we have some news for her!"

Casey winced. Charles was grinning proudly—the bad lyric had to be his idea.

Charles stepped forward with what looked like a scroll. He unraveled it to the ground, a ridiculous number of loose-leaf pages stapled end to end. "Whereas," he announced, "we the Drama Club have put our feet in mouth one too many times without watching where we've stepped—"

"Charles, that's nauseating," Reese said.

"Nobody edited this!" Brianna called out.

"And whereas," Charles continued, "we have managed, without meaning to, to chase away one of the nicest, most talented, and clear-thinking human beings in our school . . . and whereas, she has, in world-record time, proven said talent beyond a doubt and better than anyone ever seen by the gathered members hereto—"

"Herewith," Harrison corrected him.

"Herewhatever," Charles said. "We do hereby offer outright, without competition and by acclamation, to Casey Chang the position of Stage Manager of the Drama Club of Ridgeport High."

They fell silent and looked up at her with wide, tentative eyes.

One by one they dropped to their knees. "Please?" Harrison asked.

"It's the most important job in the club," Charles said. "It's the person who runs everything."

Begging. They were begging her to take this job with no experience. At *Ridgeport*. She wanted to put them on pause for a moment and think. She knew she had to say something. But to *say* something she had to *feel* something. Ecstasy, fury, amusement, *something*. She wasn't there yet. All of the thoughts raging around in her head and colliding, had somehow managed to cancel one another out.

"Thanks, guys," she said, gripping the window sash. "I'll think about it."

7

Dear Brianna,
Hey Bri!
Sup dog,
Brianna,

How are you? ~~I was wondering if~~ ~~Listen,~~ I Please
come to the projection booth ~~I have something to~~
~~show you~~ to go over problems with password protection
regarding the lighting cues.

Love,
XXXOOO,
Yours,
Sincerely,
Dashiell

"*Voilà!*"

Dashiell pointed a remote at the projection booth.

The stage, which had been bathed in white light, was now still bathed in white light.

"Okay . . . " Brianna said tentatively. "And?"

"Wait." Dashiell frowned. He took a step closer to the booth and pointed again. "*Voilà!*"

"What's supposed to happen?" Harrison asked.

"A highly dramatic lighting change," Dashiell said.

"Maybe the computer doesn't understand French," Charles remarked.

"Of course it does," Dashiell muttered. "I thought I'd conquered the learning curve on this new console. Oh well, give me a second. I will return triumphant."

"Wait—why do you need a remote?" Brianna called out. "During the show, you stay up in the booth the whole time!"

"What if there's a fire, or a gas leak, or some other emergency?" Dashiell called over his shoulder.

"But—if there's a fire—" Brianna sputtered.

But Dashiell was already heading up the aisle, mumbling technical details to himself.

"Let him be," Mr. Levin said. "We were lucky to get funding for this new console. Even luckier, they allowed overnight shipping. It's state-of-the-art. Only Broadway theaters have it better. You know Dashiell. He has to work out every last detail."

Brianna nodded, tapping her pencil on her evaluation sheets. The wall clock read 4:08. Seven minutes till callbacks.

Thirty-two kids were pacing the hallway, waiting, complaining, jabbering nervously. *It's okay,* she wanted to tell them. *Life will go on.* She knew what it was like. In her first audition, freshman year, she had been a nervous wreck. Which was so not like her. Until then *nothing* had scared her—sports, spiders, the dark, homework, Dad's brainy professor pals, Mom's rich Wall Street coworkers with their fright-mask face-lifts. Theater hadn't been on her radar screen, but Reese had been her best friend back then—and if you were Reese's friend, you auditioned. For the first time in her life, Brianna was petrified, ill with fear, *convinced* the Drama Club would throw her off the stage. To her utter shock, they cast her as Chava in *Fiddler on the Roof.* She actually cried. She was happy in a way she'd never felt before. Her parents' reaction was weird: *You're so much better than the lead girl,* they'd said. *That role was taken from you.* It took her a long time to realize that they were thinking about "her future." Lead roles *meant* something to colleges. "Bit parts" didn't. You might as well do community service or tutoring or SAT practice—all better college strategies.

Then came the *New York Times* article: "Long Island High School Breeds Broadway Babies," front page of the Sunday Arts and Leisure section, complete with a photo of the RHS's *Fiddler on the Roof.* It was instant national fame for the Drama Club—and *that,* in the eyes of the Glasers, was cool for colleges.

But Brianna never forgot the feeling. Playing Chava had rocked her world. Everything else in life was about nailing the things that "mattered"—grades, social life, extracurrics.

About being perfect. Which she'd learned how to do, with equal parts time, work, and caffeine. But the Drama Club was different. It was a place her parents couldn't touch. It was hers.

"Is Casey coming?" Harrison asked, dropping into the seat next to her.

"She wasn't at her locker this morning," Brianna replied. "I waved to her three different times in the hallway later on but didn't get a chance to talk to her. I wish I understood that girl. I mean, we handed that job to her on a plate. People would kill for that offer."

Harrison sighed. "It's all my fault. Because of my big mouth."

"You can't help it, you're Greek. You come from a long line of people who shout in diners."

"I didn't hear that ethnic slur," Harrison said, raising an eyebrow. "Well, she'll come around. Especially if she knows Kyle will be here."

"What's that supposed to mean?" Brianna asked.

"You know. She's a chick. Chicks *like* Kyle."

"Chicks," Brianna said, restraining herself, "like *corn*. Chicks like the warmth of hens—"

"Okay, okay," Harrison said with exasperation. "*Girls.*"

"Now, *girls*? They like to go to Greek diners, check out the owner's son, and order the specialty of the house . . ." A sly grin grew across her face as she balanced her clipboard shoulder height, like a waiter holding a tray.

At the sight of this transformation, Harrison bolted out of his seat. "Don't, Brianna. You know I hate that . . ."

Brianna puffed out her chest and let out a nasal taunt

that had driven him crazy since age nine. "Tseeseborger-tseeseborger-tseeseborger-tseeseborger!" she brayed, in the style of an old *Saturday Night Live* skit about Greek diners.

There was nothing Harrison hated more than being teased about his dad's diner. He was in the aisle now, backing away. "Okay, okay, I'm sorry. I admit, I'm sexist, okay?"

"Did somebody say sex?" Reese's voice, from the doorway, made them both turn.

Harrison whirled around. His mouth hung open.

"Oh. My. God," Brianna muttered.

Reese sauntered in, swaying on high-heeled dance shoes and wearing an outfit that wasted very little fabric. Her hair, brushed to a mirror sheen, hung down to her shoulders. She tossed it back, surveying the auditorium. As she moved, her cleavage took on a life of its own, the main goal of which seemed to be escaping the confines of her formfitting push-up Danskin top. "I'm ready for my close-up, Mr. DeMille."

Dashiell was walking down the aisle now, from the booth. "Um, is that *allowed*?" he asked.

"They allowed it on the cover of the July *Maxim*," Harrison remarked.

"On that model, the titties weren't real," Charles said.

"*Charles!*" Brianna gasped.

Ms. Gunderson was rushing up the aisle, holding out a white crocheted cardigan. "Darling, put this on, please."

"I don't get it," Brianna said as Ms. Gunderson led a sputtering Reese into the hallway. "That outfit—for *Godspell*?"

"It ain't for *Godspell*, darlin'," Charles said.

His eyes were fixed on the door. There was a twitter

of conversation in the hallway, and then in walked Kyle, wearing a pair of denim overalls and a faded RHS football T-shirt. "Dudes," he said in greeting.

"My day has begun," Brianna murmured.

Harrison sighed. "Chicks . . ."

"Kyle, you're number three," Brianna called out.

"Cool," Kyle said, leaping over the back of a seat so that he landed perfectly on the cushion.

"That's an interesting exercise in mechanics," Dashiell murmured.

"Don't try it," Charles said. "We don't have insurance."

By now, the other auditioners were entering. It felt different from the first day of auditions. Everyone was nervous, but the nervousness felt quieter, less deer-in the-headlights and more *focused* somehow.

"People—sign in and take seats!" Charles shouted. "Step right up, don't be shy! Remember, you're at Ridgeport High—where just making it this far is winning! I am your temporary stage manager until we find another victim—*volunteer*!"

Dashiell scurried back to the projection booth. Harrison checked his copy of the audition roster. Reese stomped back into the auditorium with a cardigan over her outfit, followed by a relieved-looking Ms. Gunderson.

Brianna kept her eye on the door, hoping to see Casey.

"'Amaaazing grace, how sweeeeeet the sound . . .'" sang Lori, her voice filling the auditorium with a sound that was glorious and huge and warm. And totally wrong for the show.

"That sounded amazing, Lori," Brianna said. "Now, please start from the beginning—only pretend that you're speaking to me in a conversation. I mean, sing, but don't *think* about singing. The notes will take care of themselves. Think of the words instead. Like they just popped into your head for the first time. From the heart. So, tell me—what's so amazing about grace?"

Lori looked puzzled for a moment. "It's a religious song. About, like, finding God and being saved? Isn't *Godspell* religious?"

"Right. So, tell me about that sweet sound! What did it do to you? Talk to me."

Lori swallowed. She looked a little scared. "It—it saved a wretch . . . like me," she said, reciting the lyric. "Brianna, this is embarrassing."

"Go on . . ."

Lori closed her eyes and breathed deeply. Softly Ms. Gunderson started to play. Lori began to sing again, starting in a low, tentative voice full of wonder and tenderness. Her body tipped slightly forward as if in prayer, and her voice grew with emotion. Brianna listened, and this time, all she could think of was *yes*. She wasn't hearing Big Voice. She was seeing a joyous girl saved from a life of suffering. The song wasn't just words anymore. It was a story set to music.

When it was over, Ms. Gunderson had to wipe a tear from her cheek.

"Thank you, Lori," Brianna said.

She stole a glance at Harrison. He smiled.

"Amazing," Charles whispered. "Brianna Glaser.

Actress. Singer. Inspiration to the Multitudes. Is there nothing she can't do?"

Okay, the technique didn't always work. Jason Riddick had a sweet voice—but when Brianna asked him to "speak," he spoke. And then he sang out of tune.

Reese danced and sang like a star, which surprised no one. She also tore off her cardigan toward the end of her audition, which brought a huge round of applause. And also surprised no one.

Corbin, who was one of the school's best singers, looked scared and small onstage—until Harrison called up Ethan to join him. A double audition was completely against the rules, Brianna pointed out. But the two guys were incredible together, singing "Anything You Can Do, I Can Do Better" while doing magic tricks onstage. One point for Harrison.

When Kyle's name was called, the auditorium fell dead silent. They all waited, but no one came through the door.

"Kyle?" Harrison repeated. "Hello?"

"He's not here," someone called from the hallway.

Brianna sprang out of her seat. "What do you mean, *not here*?"

She ran into the hallway, asked where Kyle was. Nothing but shrugs, *duh*-filled eyes. No one knew where he was. She ran out the school door, sprinted around the building and onto the playing field.

Kyle was limping quickly across the grass, looking up and over his shoulder—and heading straight for the fence. A football was bulleting toward him. "KYLE!" Brianna called out.

He glanced at her. The football hit him in the shoulder. As he tried to avoid the fence, his ankle buckled beneath him. He lurched forward, hit the fence, and fell.

Brianna ran toward him. "Are you okay?"

"I'm cool," he said, struggling to his feet. "Did the tryout start already? Damn. I thought I had some time. *Yo, yo, dudes! I gotta go! Be back later!*"

He put an arm around her shoulder and hobbled back into the school, letting go of her only when they got to the auditorium. Apologizing to everyone, he limped down the aisle and climbed onstage. His overalls were caked with mud. He had a cut on one cheek.

Brianna took a seat next to Charles. "The soiled look is all over the Paris runways this season," he said.

"Shut up and listen," Brianna said.

"Hello, Kyle," Ms. Gunderson asked. "May I have your music?"

"*Music?*" Kyle's face fell. "Crap, it's outside."

"We don't have time for this," Harrison grumbled. "If he knew he was supposed to sing—"

Brianna ran to the piano and leafed through the stack of Ms. Gunderson's music. She read off a list of songs, tunes she knew Kyle could handle: "Sit Down, You're Rocking the Boat" from *Guys and Dolls*, "Almost Like Being in Love" from *Brigadoon*, "Bring Him Home" from *Les Misérables*.

He didn't know any of them.

"I thought your mom listened to show tunes," Brianna said.

Kyle smiled. "Doesn't mean I know them all. Most of them kind of suck, you gotta admit."

"What *do* you know?" Brianna asked.

"'Danny Boy'?" he said sheepishly. "My dad sings that, like, seventeen times a day."

Immediately Ms. Gunderson began playing the intro. Brianna crossed her fingers.

"'O Danny Boy, the pipes, the pipes are falling . . .'" he began.

The correct word was *calling*. But it didn't matter. Kyle sang the song with style. And no mistakes. And he made Charles cry.

They gave him "sides"—sections of the play's dialogue. He read them without any preparation. He was a natural actor, Brianna noticed. Funny, warm, comfortable in his body. And he could sense wherever Dashiell's spotlight was. It was something not every person could do—half the time kids would just walk into a shadow and not know it. But Kyle had that ability to "find the heat." Wherever the light was, there was his face.

Damn. Damn. Damn. It was at times like this that she regretted deciding to be student director. If she had been allowed to audition, she would be *playing opposite him.* The possibilities would have been endless.

"I can't take my eyes off him," Brianna whispered to Charles.

"You're not the only one," he replied, gesturing toward stage right.

Reese, her cardigan abandoned, was walking onstage. With a big smile, she sidled up close to Kyle. "If y'all don't mind, I'd like to put him through a simple dance routine."

"Uh, 'y'all'?" Charles said. "Since when did we become Southern?"

"Look at her body language," Harrison said with disgust.

"She might as well thrust them in his face."

"I can hear you, you know," Reese said. "Now, Kyle, can you do this? Sidestep, kick-step-kick." She demonstrated a dance step that was all chest thrusts and hip wiggles, ending up right next to Kyle with her chest positioned so that his eyes could not help but go south.

When Kyle tried the dance step, with the same thrusts and wiggles, the whole auditorium burst into hysterics.

Kyle grinned at Reese. Reese scowled.

Yes, he was a keeper.

Brianna's only regret was that she couldn't be onstage, acting and singing next to him. That hurt.

Then again, she'd be able to tell him what to do. There were some definite advantages to that.

8

Journal
Kara Chang
Thursday, September 13

Callbacks are happening now, and I am at home. This is because I am such a jerk. Number One, I closed the window on the only people I know in this school when they were being nice to me, which was rude, dumb, and immature. I could have invited them in, or at least talked to them. Number Two, I didn't apologize to Brianna about it. Yesterday, I was still too freaked to say anything. But I MEANT to do it this morning at the lockers and would have if MOM hadn't burned cranberry pancakes for breakfast and insisted on making another batch, making me almost late for school, despite the fact that I HATE cranberry pancakes but ONE TIME when I was six or seven I must have said "Yum" when I saw a plate of them, so she somehow thinks they're my favorite food ever and she made them especially for me because she sensed I was upset—and how can she be so wrong about one thing and so right about the other? But this is typical of Casey the Coward. I can't tell Mom the truth about this, ever, and then when I finally arrive at school late and have to go straight to homeroom and miss my morning locker-time with Brianna, I totally chicken out and can't say a word to her the WHOLE DAY LONG and by the end of the day I figure the Drama Club is pissed at me anyway so even if I begged to be involved, why on earth would they want me?

Well, I blew my chance. Stage managering would have been nice. Maybe someday I can at least make friends with them. If they don't totally think I'm scum.

I just ate a whole pint of Haagen-Dazs Dulce de Leche ice cream. Mom's working at the hospital so she wasn't here to stop me. That's another thing. I'm fat. Since we moved here, I can't stop eating. Maybe if I stay away from the Drama Club, I'll have time to concentrate on losing weight.

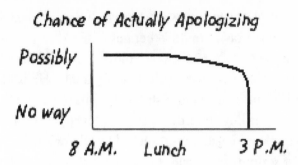

Chance of Actually Apologizing

Possibly

No way

8 A.M.   Lunch   3 P.M.

It was cold, way too cold for the time of the year. Casey's teeth chattered as she rushed toward school in the setting sun. If she believed in divine retribution, this would be the right punishment for her behavior.

Rounding the corner of the auto-body shop, Casey saw the back of the school. The parking lot, just beyond the playing field, was still fairly full, and she thought she could spot Mr. Levin's beat-up old Taurus. Good. Maybe they were still there.

To shore up her nerves, she took out her cell phone and looked at Brianna's text message:

WE ♥ YOU PLS COME AFTER CALLBAX IF U WANT @ 5:30 WE COULD USE SOME HELP.

It was now 5:47. She would have been there earlier, but she picked up the message only a few moments ago. It was that kind of day.

"He goes back to pass!" a voice yelled.

Walking with her head down, Casey hadn't paid much attention to the guys playing touch football on the field.

She looked up to see Kyle Taggart limping backward toward her, away from the other guys.

"Excuse me!" she called out, moving to avoid him.

But he was fast, even with the bum ankle. He backed right into her, and before she had a chance to scream, she was hurtling toward the ground, wrapped in a pair of long, flannel-clad arms. "Sacked by Chang behind the line of scrimmage!" Kyle shouted, falling to the ground and pulling her on top of him.

Casey let out a scream of surprise. "Kyyyyyle!"

"Flag on the play!" he bellowed. "Chang will not let go, ladies and gentlemen! She's tough! She's brutal! The crowd goes wild!"

He was on his back, holding her above him, rolling from side to side. He was gentle, playful, not what she would have expected. She was in *Kyle Taggart's* arms and the fact made her giggle helplessly. Kyle finally rolled them both to a sitting position and feigned exhaustion and defeat.

The other guys, Kyle's friends, were averting their eyes impatiently and snickering. "Come on, Taggart!" one of the other guys called out.

"I'm on the temporary disabled list!" Kyle shouted back, tossing them the football. He smiled at Casey. "Sorry, couldn't resist."

She brushed herself off, feeling as if the earth had tilted back in the other direction and it was now mid-August and her fall jacket was making her way, way too hot, while the words "couldn't resist" rolled around in her head with all the hints of possibility. "No problem. Um, how did you do this afternoon?"

"In tryouts?" he asked.

"Callbacks. Not tryouts."

Kyle shrugged. "I don't know. They didn't throw anything at me. You?"

He had no clue about his talent. She looked into those big-sky eyes and that fearless smile. Absurd as it seemed, this guy who could tackle a strange girl on a dirty field and make her feel good about it, who could tuck an auditorium full of theater geeks into his back pocket, who could throw a football like a bullet, *had no clue.*

"I didn't get a callback," Casey said lamely, checking her watch. "I'm just visiting. Well, uh, good luck."

"Later!"

As he limped back to his friends, Casey ran toward the school. Her legs weren't feeling too steady either. She gripped the handle of the back entrance and pulled the door open.

Brianna was standing on the other side. "Boo," she said with a startled laugh. "Hey, you're here! You got my text message! I'm *so* glad you came." She took Casey's arm. "We already picked the cast. Want to see the list? Listen, there's a lot you can do to help out. The others will be thrilled—"

"No, wait," Casey said. "I don't want to see everybody yet. Can we talk, just you and me?"

Brianna let go. She gave Casey a curious look, then smiled. "I am all about talk. My car is in the lot. The red Camry."

Casey blanched. She hadn't anticipated this. "Wait. I was thinking we'd walk somewhere—"

"We'll walk when we get to the mall," Brianna said.

"Mall?"

"You are in for the treat of a lifetime. You're going shopping with me."

She was nervous. Brianna noticed it right away.

On the drive to the parkway entrance, she had given Casey the final cast list and schedule: Kyle as Jesus, Harrison as John the Baptist/Judas, Lori as the "Day by Day" soloist, and Reese, Corbin, Ethan, Jamil, Lynnette, Aisha, and Becky as the other disciples. Rehearsals to begin Monday, September 17, performances November 16 and 17. It all seemed to go in one ear and out the other. Except for the news about Kyle. Casey had seemed interested in that. Judging from the little incident on the football field, which Brianna had seen through the window, Casey had fallen for him like everyone else.

Brianna put down the windows. Patches of brown and yellow mottled the trees, and if you tried hard enough you could detect a faint salty whiff of the ocean. It didn't help. Casey looked like she hadn't ever been in a car before. Her right hand gripped the door handle, her right leg was rigid against the floor. She had barely said a word, and now they were already onto the parkway, halfway to the mall. As Brianna signaled and slipped into the center lane, she noticed Casey peering at the speedometer. Seventy-six miles an hour. Oops. Okay, that was a bit much. Brianna eased up on the accelerator.

"I hope you're not expecting the Mall of America," Brianna said. "Taft Field is like the world's first mall or something. I think Cleopatra used to shop there. They've fixed it up, though—you *can't* really be a Long Islander until you've shopped at Taft Field. And besides, you're going to need some power clothes if you plan to be stage manager."

"Huh?" Casey finally looked at her. "Stage manager? You still want me to do that?"

"Do you want to?"

Casey looked stunned. "Well, the reason I came to school was to apologize. I was mean to you the other day."

"Apology accepted!" Brianna said. "Now, let's discuss the pros and cons of being a stage manager. First the pros. One: You're perfect. Two: Everybody loves you. Three: You can do this job—it's mostly just holding the clipboard with the schedule on it, and making sure people stay on track during the rehearsal. Four: If you say no, poor Charles will have a heart attack. Now for the cons. Wait . . . ummmm. Well, I can't think of any cons, can you?"

Casey didn't answer for a long time. "It's a lot of responsibility," she finally said. "So much that can go wrong."

"It's a *show*, Casey. It's not football or lacrosse or hockey, where you can get your kishkes knocked out."

"Kishkes? What does that mean?"

"I'm not sure. It's something Vijay says. It's Yiddish."

"Isn't he Indian?"

"Yes. You see what a bunch of eccentric and interesting people we have?"

Casey sighed. "People can get injured onstage. Props can break and cut people. Turntables can trap shoelaces and mangle people's feet. I read about someone whose jaw had to be wired after she ran into another actor in the dark. I would be responsible for the safety of everyone. I don't know if I can trust myself."

Trust myself? Brianna had to look at her to make sure this wasn't a joke. It wasn't. This was too lame. Maybe Casey was afraid of something. Somehow the football incident with Kyle came to mind. "Can I ask you a personal question? Is this about Kyle?"

"*Kyle?* Not at all."

"Is it the time commitment? Because I totally understand that. There are ways to get your homework done. All of us do really well in school, especially Harrison. Well, me, too. My parents will disown me if I don't go to Yale. Which is fine with me, because afterward I can go to Yale Drama School. I'll have six APs, and if I can keep my average above a ninety-six and crack a twenty-three hundred, maybe twenty-three fifty on the SATs, plus community service, school radio station, and orchestra—"

"Wow," Casey said. "Do you ever sleep?"

Brianna hated that question. It sounded like her mother speaking. "I sleep enough. Some people don't need much sleep."

Through her left window, Brianna saw a massive Hummer heading into her lane. She leaned on the horn and swerved to the right.

"Watch it!" Casey yelled.

WHAAAAAA! The driver of the car to the right of them leaned on his horn.

The Hummer lurched back into its lane. A scornful face

appeared in the passenger's-side window, accompanied by a flipped middle finger.

"*He* does the wrong thing and then abuses *me?*" Brianna leaned on her horn again. "*Hey, you're two for two—you destroy the environment AND you're ugly!*"

The Hummer braked and started to slow down. Its passenger's-side window slid open.

"*Brianna, don't!*" Casey shrieked.

"Yeeps, road rage, time to book," Brianna said. The exit for Taft Field was just ahead. She got into the right lane, signaled, took the ramp off the highway, and slowed to a smooth stop at a red light. "Well. That was exciting."

Casey was staring straight ahead. Her eyes were wide, her skin pale. Beads of sweat clung to her forehead.

"Hey, are you all right?" Brianna asked.

"Fine," Casey said, mopping her forehead with the back of her hand. "Let's just park and get out of the car."

Brianna nodded. The light turned green. Another car blared its horn. Brianna glanced in the rearview mirror but did not respond.

Turning left, she drove to the mall. Casey was still clutching the armrest, at twenty-six miles per hour. Brianna wanted to scream.

In the parking lot, a bus was unloading white-haired ladies in pantsuits at the mall entrance. Brianna bit her lip, pulled into a spot, and managed not to ask Casey if she wanted to join them for the ride home.

9

YaLeBiRd: *BRI, I GOT IT! I AM STAGE MGRING A PLAYYY!!!!!!*

YaLeBiRd: *called caucasian chalk circle*

dramakween: woo-hoooo rachel kolodzny is hot. watch out yale!!! never hoid of ccc. is it like harold & the purple crayon?

dramakween: that would make a good play.

YaLeBiRd: *maybe in 2 years, when ur here*

dramakween: *lol*

dramakween: hey, guess what! we found a new sm!

YaLeBiRd: *whaaaat??? you replaced me? impossible! ☺ rofl . . .*

dramakween: well shes not as brainy and bootilicious as you.

dramakween: in fact, shes a little weird. i thought she was going to turn us down.

YaLeBiRd: is she crazy??? what did you do??????

dramakween: took her to taft field, bought her clothes, fed her a mochacino (sp?) and brownie and half of my carrot cake.

YaLeBiRd: then she said yes? because of carrot cake?

dramakween: nope. she kept saying no. i couldn't believe it.

dramakween: i tried to act like siobhan the super-nanny. the way she deals with colter when he's annoying. She just listens.

dramakween: so i listened. and listened and listened.

YaLeBiRd: mmmm

dramakween: she sez she has this fear of cars, & that explained her behavior, i guess. casey, not siobhan.

dramakween: big tearfest. she was all wound up about it.

dramakween: then she said yes. tada. instant sm!

YaLeBiRd: uh-huh. so ur happy?

dramakween: yes!!!! can u imagine no sm? charles was gonna have a heart attack.

YaLeBiRd: congratz. but

YaLeBiRd: FEAR OF CARS? where does she come from? jupiter?

dramakween: i know. my B.S. meter goes wild with this girl. i dont know why . . .

YaLeBiRd: *b careful*

dramakween: u know me. caution is my middle name.

dramakween: gotta go. lurve & kishkes . . .

"Crap!" said Corbin, throwing his script to the main stage floor. "I'm sorry. I'm sorry!"

"Language, plee-ee-eease!" Ms. Gunderson sang out sweetly from her seat at the piano.

"I'm not feeling it," Corbin fumed. "I'm supposed to be funny, but I'm not funny. Can I use an accent?"

Sitting in the fifth row next to Casey, Brianna massaged her forehead.

"Should you give him direction?" Casey asked.

"I will," Brianna said. "After Mr. Levin gets through with him."

She missed acting. When you were onstage, you could ignore other people's neuroses. When you were a director, they were rubbed in your face.

From the row behind them, Dashiell leaned forward. He had been hanging around Brianna all day, promising to give her something but never doing it or even saying what it was. Then again, Dashiell was the last of the absentminded geniuses. "Interesting," he remarked. "I guess you can't always predict which of the cast members will emerge as the diva."

"They usually emerge *after* the first rehearsal," Brianna said, "not during."

The other actors were gathered in a circle at center stage, standing around Reese, who was wearing a bright blue French-cut leotard and trying to demonstrate a dance move. She strutted across the stage, took Corbin by his shirt collar, and dragged him into the circle. "Corbin, we just *had* a read-through. We're not running lines right now. We are dancing. Exploring our psychedelic inner seventies flower children! Now, loosen up. Hippify yourself!"

Brianna watched in disbelief as the actors began jumping around the stage with huge smiles, arms flailing, eyes wide.

" 'Hippify'?" Casey said.

"Reese's concept for the show is 'Hippie Potfest meets Medieval Morality Play,' " Brianna said. "She picked up that last phrase on Google. She's trying to impress Harrison."

"I see," Casey said. "Well, they look . . . energetic."

"They look like they just escaped from the loony bin," Brianna added.

"Have you seen the movie? They looked the same way." Dashiell shrugged. "It's quite fun to watch. All the Afros flying around."

"So maybe our cast, their hair looks . . . I don't know . . . too twenty-first century?" Casey said. "Maybe we could work on that, I think."

"What are you suggesting?" Brianna said. "Hair doesn't grow that much in two months."

"Right. You're right," Casey said. "But there are wigs? You know, seventies-style wigs? We had a theatrical-wig store where I used to live. I'm sure we could find one here . . . "

Brianna laughed, picturing Harrison with an Afro.

"Might work. I like it. And yeah, there is a shop in Ridgeport on Sunrise Highway. It's called Hair Today, Gone Tomorrow. I don't know the phone number."

"Brianna, that's an excellent idea!" Dashiell exclaimed. "You're a certified genius."

"It was Casey's idea," Brianna said.

"I'll call." Casey scribbled something on a sheet of paper. "Oh—Dashiell! The school has Wi-Fi, right? What if you rigged the new lighting computer to it? If I keep a laptop backstage, we could network them and both work the cues."

Dashiell nodded. "Depends on the software. I'll check."

"Great." Casey stood up, pulled a cell phone out of her pocket, and made her way across the seats toward the aisle. "Ridgeport, please. The number for Hair Today, Gone Tomorrow . . ."

"She is the bomb," Dashiell said, but his approving grin quickly vanished. "I mean, after you. You have, um, the greater bombness." He edged toward the aisle. "I'll . . . go check the software now . . . "

Brianna watched him go. Lately, Dashiell had been acting like this a lot. Maybe he was crushing on Casey. . . .

Casey was impressing everyone. She was sharp. She had spine behind that timid exterior. Mr. Levin was beaming. Charles was in raptures. She even forced Dashiell into grammar hell.

Could this possibly be the same person? Casey obviously had had some leadership experience somewhere. But Brianna didn't ever remember her talking about it.

Which was weird. Wouldn't it be one of the *first* topics of conversation?

"Peace and love!" came Kyle's voice from the stage. "Make love, not war!"

"Kyle, put me down!"

Brianna looked up. Kyle had lifted Lori high over his head and was trying to get her to sit on his shoulders. Brianna fought back the pit-of-the-stomach feeling that said, *That could have been me.*

Lori, however, looked scared.

"Cut!" Reese called out. "Stop!"

"Let her down, Kyle," Mr. Levin called out, standing at the lip of the stage. "Look, guys, this play is not just goofy movement, dumb jokes, and nice songs. It's not *That '70s Show.* It *means* something."

"Godspell means Gospel," Lori volunteered. "Good news."

"We're supposed to be like a band of brothers and sisters," Becky spoke up. "Sharing stuff."

"Stuff?" Mr. Levin said. "What stuff?"

"Love . . . " Jamil mumbled. "Faith?"

"Yes!" Mr. Levin replied, leaping onstage. "Also truth and fun and uncorrupted youth—all those things in the middle of a loveless world. The first part of the play is triumphant. Innocent. Trusting. Joyous."

"Woo-hoooo!" Kyle shouted, kicking his good leg into the air. "Dudes. God save the people . . . et cetera!"

"As Jesus, you enter in the middle of the first number, Kyle," Mr. Levin said. "And you enter as a child. A representation of purity and goodness. Until your baptism, you are shirtless and shoeless."

"Shirtless?" Kyle said, dropping to the floor and doing push-ups. "Gotta work on my pecs. One . . . two . . . three . . ."

Reese began fanning herself. "I think I'm going to have a stroke."

"Kyle, please . . . " Mr. Levin said. "Pay attention."

Charles noticed he wasn't sneezing anymore. That was a good sign. It meant the paint in the costume/prop room was finally dry. Not that you could even *see* the paint job. The shelves were crammed full, and the remaining wall space was covered by file cabinets, stacked boxes, and racks. Even the revered poster of the Ridgeport High production of *Into the Woods* autographed by Stephen Sondheim (comment: "One of the best productions I have seen. Period.") was temporarily put into storage. It had all happened so fast—Mr. Ippolito had had the room replastered and painted over the weekend, and Casey and the Charlettes had stacked everything before homeroom and during lunch and study halls today, Monday.

Charles went back to his task, typing labels into the database on his laptop. Casey had bought adhesive labels, and as soon as he printed them out, every single item would be labeled, categorized, inventoried. Charles was sure that Ridgeport's props had never come close to being this organized.

Casey was awesome, and he worshipped her.

Vijay stuck his head in from the hallway. "The goddess has arrived."

As Casey walked in, Charles grabbed a rubber chicken from the shelf and fell to his knees. "O Savior of the Stage, we give this offering in gratitude and awe."

"Stop," Casey said, turning deep red. "Um, I just wanted to ask, can we make some extra space? We're getting wigs. Like Victor Garber's Afro in the movie? Very seventies. The wig shop is giving us two of them, three sets of pigtails, and a ponytail. They wanted to charge, but I offered them a full-page ad in the program instead. I hope that's okay?"

"Casey, *you* are the boss—of course it's okay! You go, girl!" Charles said. "How's the rehearsal going?"

Casey sat. "Well, I don't like to talk behind people's backs . . ."

"Darlin', backstage is made for gossip," Charles replied. "Either you start now or I will have to train you."

"Okay. Um, well . . . " Casey furrowed her brow thoughtfully, as if in the middle of an exam. "Kyle's doing push-ups. Corbin seems troubled. Reese's clothes are falling off. Ethan seems to be in slow motion. And Harrison's on the verge of a heart attack."

"Ha! You're *good* at this!" Charles cried out, clapping his hands. "Okay, these are good signs. They mean the show will be fantastic. Bad rehearsal, great show—the old saying. But no matter what, remember, the Charlettes will make sure it all looks fabulous."

Casey glanced at a sheet of paper on the table, where Charles had drawn a sketch of the Jesus character, dressed in a Superman T-shirt and bound by red ribbons to a chain-link fence. "What's this?" Casey asked.

"The crucifixion scene," Charles replied. "Jesus on the fence. I'm thinking lots of red, flowing ribbons, bright and symbolic without being gory . . . "

"Do we have a fence?"

"The Charlettes will paint a backdrop."

Casey thought a moment then smiled. "I have an idea. Can I show you?"

"I am your acolyte," Charles said.

She stood and led Charles into the hallway. They hurried down a corridor to the school's rear exit, which led outside to a dark, fenced-in area where the trash was stored in three large Dumpsters. Construction debris was piled against the wall, casting ominous shadows.

"If you want to make out with me, Casey," Charles said, "I can think of a few sexier spots. Like behind the steam tables in the cafeteria."

Casey blushed. Turning away from him, she leaned over a pile of bricks and rattled a chain-link fence. It was enormous, at least ten feet high. "I was thinking . . . maybe this is a dumb idea . . . do you think we can get this into the wings?"

Charles glanced from the fence to the small school entrance door. "Uh . . . no, it's not a dumb idea. In fact, I thought of it myself. I even talked to Mr. Ippolito about it, but he didn't like the idea. And I think he was right. I took a closer look and I was like, 'Gah, what are you *thinking?*' (A) It's filthy and rusty, and (B) it would stain the costumes, and (C) I doubt the school has insurance against gangrene, and (D) it would never fit through the door, and (F) it weighs a ton."

"You skipped E."

"I'll think of something."

"Look, we could clean off the rust," Casey said. "There are products for that. And it would look perfect. . . ."

"You want to try Mr. Ippolito again? Be my guest. But

take some NoDoz before you go. Unless you're dying to hear about his experience as the Tree in *The Wizard of Oz* in 1492. Look, doll, the Charlettes have great artistic abilities. At least I hope they do."

"They do," Casey agreed. "But the fence would be more realistic."

"No offense—ha, that's a pun—but don't get grandiose. It can backfire on you. Personally, I like that in a girl. You remind me of me, which is one of the reasons I see Dr. Fink. He specializes in grandiose teenagers. Now I have to get back. You do what you need to do."

"Okay," Casey said, a little baffled. Sometimes she wasn't sure what Charles was talking about. "See you in the auditorium."

Mr. Ippolito, the janitor, leaned back, putting his feet on the cracked Formica desk. "Yeah, Chasey, you're gonna love it here."

"Casey," Casey said gently.

"I used to be an actor in this high school, too, y'know. Yep." He leaned forward meaningfully, as if to give his words proper weight. "I played the role of Cord Elam. In *Oklahoma!* I *owned* Cord Elam. You know the role?"

Casey nodded. She'd never heard of it. "That's so great. So you really *understand* us. The custodian in my old school? He wouldn't let us use a stepladder in *Carousel—*"

Mr. Ippolito sat bolt upright. "For the Starkeeper? You *gotta* have a ladder for that scene."

"He banned plastic retractable knives for *West Side Story.*"

"Awww, no!" Mr. Ippolito groaned. "What'd he expect the actors to do, slap each other to death?"

"I'm glad we didn't do *Godspell* there . . ." Casey's heart was fluttering so hard, she was sure he could tell. She wasn't used to doing this kind of thing, but gentle prodding was not nearly as bad as lying, and she had been doing a lot of that lately. If she could get Mr. Ippolito invested in the idea of *the best possible play* . . . "He would never have let us build realistic scenes. Like in the crucifixion . . ."

"That's a *great* scene! The movie, with the cop cars in the background, Judas selling him out . . ."

Casey swallowed hard. "I know Charles has already asked you about the fence outside?"

"In the back? Yeah, but he didn't mention what it was for."

"It's an amazing scene . . ."

"Very dramatic," Mr. Ippolito said, tapping his fingers on the desk. "The climax, if you will."

"I think if we fixed it up a bit, got rid of the rust . . ."

Mr. Ippolito sat back, mulling it over. For a long time he didn't say a word. "I wanted them to use a real surrey in *Oklahoma!*, and a real horse. I knew where to get them. A real show horse, one that wouldn't mess up the stage or freak out. But they wouldn't let me do it. They used that stupid cardboard . . ."

His voice trailed off, and he suddenly sat forward. "You know something, Kathy? I'm going to go to bat for you on this one. Let me take a look at it and figure out the best strategy . . ."

He leaped from his chair and opened the door for Casey.

As she walked out, she spotted Charles. He had been standing just outside the door, and he must have been listening in, because his face showed utter disbelief.

10

From: <harrison.michaels@rport.li.com>
To: <stavrosdagreek@nyc.cable.net>
Subject: lost in ny???
September 21, 6:32 P.M.

Stavros,

When are you gonna be back on the buddy list? Are you getting these e-mails? Let me hear from you. How's the new apartment? Papou and Yiayia can't wrap their minds around the fact that you moved from Long Island to "Brooklee." They think all moves are supposed to happen the other way around. I think they feel sorry for you.

Oh, guess what? I am playing Judas in Godspell.

It's the lead. He doubles with John the Baptist.
The alpha and the omega. I love playing bad guys,
mwah-ha-ha. It's a much better role than Jesus.

I'll send jpegs.

H

"Hold it right there!" Ms. Gunderson said. "Kyle,
you have to sing while you do the soft-shoe. You
can't let Harrison do it all. This is a huge number, a
showstopper."

Kyle grimaced as he set down his rolled-up umbrella.
He and Harrison were supposed to be using canes, but the
canes hadn't arrived yet from the supplier. "Yeah. Sorry.
It's the ankle."

"Are you going to be okay?" Reese the Patient
Choreographer asked. "Because we can change the
number and make it easier."

"Nah, I'll get it," Kyle replied. "I'm a football guy.
Football is all about managing pain."

"And knowing left from right," Harrison added.

Kyle grinned. "Dude."

"Okay, then," Reese said, "now remember, swing the
cane to the right first, *then* move your left leg. If you get
it wrong, you will kick Harrison and knock him off the
platform. And we don't want to see *either* of you guys
injured and bedridden. Well, injured."

Backstage, Casey drummed her fingers on the wooden
surface of the school lectern, where her laptop was set
up. She fiddled with her IM settings, hoping Dashiell had

finally figured out how to get his lighting-board computer onto the wireless network.

She loved watching the rehearsal from the wings. The best part was seeing Kyle sing. From the side, you didn't have to worry about his noticing you watch him.

" 'All for the Best,' from the top," Ms. Gunderson said. "One, two, three, four . . . "

Harrison and Kyle jumped into place on a narrow platform. They grabbed top hats like two vaudeville performers. Two rolled-up umbrellas materialized out of nowhere. Casey grinned.

"Now . . . kickline!" Reese cried out.

Harrison lifted his hat and kicked sharply, crisply to the right.

Kyle kicked to the left.

"Yeoowww!" Harrison fell to the stage, clutching his ankle.

"Crap!" Kyle said, throwing his hat to the floor in frustration. "Sorry about that."

"No problem, I have another one," Harrison said bravely.

"Break!" Ms. Gunderson called out. "Kyle, may I work with you alone, please?"

As the actors headed offstage, Harrison struggled to his feet, gave Kyle a supportive thumbs-up, and fell in step with Ethan. "Let us gather like sheep, not goats, fellow traveler!" he said, clapping his arm wearily around Ethan's shoulder.

"Will you knock it off?" Ethan said.

Harrison was the kind of actor who liked to stay in

character offstage. He also liked to give advice. Casey had seen him teaching Kyle to make gorilla noises and walk with his arms scraping the floor, insisting that this would help his acting skills. Casey wasn't sure it really helped.

Now he was talking to Ethan. For all four days of rehearsal, Ethan had been lifeless, mumbling his line readings and songs. The two guys were speaking softly, until finally Ethan exploded: "Um, wait. Are *you* the student director? Huh? Are you? Levin and Brianna *both* know what I'm doing." With that, he turned and walked offstage.

Brianna, noticing the commotion, had come backstage. She, Reese, and Harrison all converged at Casey's station. "Hey, student director, can we replace that jerk?" Harrison said to Brianna.

Reese nodded. "I agree. You know what he tells me? He's 'marking.' He says a good actor doesn't go all out at the beginning. That's 'unprofessional.' You have to rein it in. Explore the inner life of the character slowly . . . "

"Slowly? He's comatose!" Harrison said.

"Harrison," Brianna said patiently, "you know you're not allowed to direct and act in the same play. Don't worry. We're on him. We'll talk to him again."

They all turned to the stage as Kyle began singing "God Save the People," and hitting a few clams until Ms. Gunderson stopped him. "Sweetie, your sound is amazing," she said. "Just one teeny thing—the high note is an E-flat, remember? You're singing the wrong note on the word *save*."

"He's having a rough day; let's give him some props,"

Brianna whispered. Then she called out to the stage, "You sound fantastic, Kyle! Beautiful tone."

"Excellent!" Harrison agreed.

Kyle turned with a start, not used to hearing their voices from stage right. He smiled and gave a devil-may-care shrug. He didn't look insecure, but he had to be feeling it.

As he began singing again, Reese sighed. "Can you believe the size of that thing?"

Brianna nodded. "It's a major voice."

"Unless you were referring to something else," Harrison said.

"You have a one-track mind," Reese replied.

"*I* do? Why don't you just go up there and grab him?" Harrison asked. "Maybe *then* he'd reach the high notes."

Reese raised an eyebrow. "Honey, you are just jealous, because the biggest basket in *your* life is filled with bread. *Yia soo*, Greek boy."

Harrison turned away. "It's Be Snarky to Harrison Day," he said over his shoulder.

Casey noticed some movement on her laptop. A message from Dashiell.

Let_there_be_light: zzzup sistah

Nice. Finally! Casey quickly typed a response:

changchangchang: you did it!!! the wifi works! geeks rule!!!!!!!!!!!!!!

"Woo-hoo!" came Dashiell's voice from the lighting booth, distracting everybody.

changchangchang: ssshhhhhhh
Let_there_be_light: sorry

Casey shut her laptop and stood by the edge of the stage. To her left, behind the curtains, Corbin and Ethan were playing a card game while reciting lines. Onstage, Mr. Levin had finished giving Kyle "notes"—criticisms—on his singing. Casey quickly checked her rehearsal sheet and said, "*Cast! Listen up!* Everyone onstage for 'Day by Day'!"

"I was going to give a few more notes," Mr. Levin said with a patient smile.

Casey checked her watch. "Can you do it afterward? We're off schedule."

What are you doing? screamed Casey's brain. *Talking back to the director is not kosher. Not not not. Ease up. It's happening. That old feeling—you can do anything, nothing touches you. That feeling you paid for last year by screwing up everything.*

But Mr. Levin didn't seem mad, just amused. "Sure, Casey," he said. "You're right, actually."

Now Charles came popping out of the wings. "Okay, kids, imagine a junkyard—a colorful Disneyworld of cool props you can use to act out the gospel lessons—umbrellas, baby carriages, a scooter, a wagon . . ."

Casey watched, letting her brain cool down. The scene unfolded, soon leading into the song "Day by Day," Lori's solo. Casey's IM chime interrupted the mood. Stepping back, she glanced at the screen.

Let_there_be_light: links done. wanna try Cue 57A & see if it works?

She typed back

changchangchang: *sure*

Accessing the site, she quickly entered her user name and password. All the cues were lined up in numerical order with descriptions. Casey clicked on "57A: Day by Day 1."

In an instant the stage went dark except for a circle of light focused only on Kyle and Lori. They seemed suspended in a perfect white globe. Casey shot a thumbs-up to Dashiell, who was dancing in the booth.

Then she braced herself for the song. That phrase—*day by day*—still cut to the bone. After the hospital, that's what they had told her: take it day by day, and things would get better. Of course, it wasn't true. When she got home, when she found out what had really happened, she knew that it could never get better. Not day by day, not as long as she lived.

Lori's voice soared as she sang "these things I pray," and Casey's memories faded as she imagined trading places, so *she* would be touching Kyle's fingers, one by one.

"Pssst!" From the rear exit, out past the costume/prop room, Charles waved Casey toward him. She ran to the door. It was open, and loud angry voices filtered in. One of them was Mr. Ippolito's.

Casey peeked out to see him standing face-to-face with the principal of the school, Ms. Hecksher. "If in my judgment this were unsafe," Mr. Ippolito was saying, "you can be sure I would not do it!"

"The issues here are not only safety," Ms. Hecksher

snapped, "but cleanliness, protection of property, and respect for process! And beyond that, Mr. Ippolito, there are *guidelines*. Unless your job description and union affiliation have changed drastically since I last checked, you are *not* the faculty adviser to the Drama Club!"

Casey looked past Ms. Hecksher and saw what she was upset about. At the end of the hallway, cushioned by thick rags, the enormous rust-covered chain-link fence leaned against the wall.

Charles came up behind Casey. "*We have to do something!*" he whispered.

Before she could say a word, Mr. Levin came toward them. "Is there a problem?"

Mr. Ippolito began explaining that because he was a huge *Godspell* fan, he had come up with the idea to bring in the fence for the junkyard scenes.

He was taking the fall. Putting his job on the line. Not even mentioning that it *hadn't been* his idea.

"Um . . . " Casey said. "I . . . it was my . . . "

Nobody was listening. A crowd was gathering around her, curious actors and the Charlettes. Mr. Levin turned to them wearily and said, "People, let's take a fifteen-minute break."

"Mr. Levin," Casey pressed on, "I was the one who wanted the fence."

"Um, if you're looking for martyrs, add little old *moi*," Charles piped up. "I planted the stupid idea—"

"Casey, Charles, please, you are not employees of the school," Mr. Levin replied. "Let Ms. Hecksher deal with this."

"B-but—" Casey stammered.

The crowd was pushing her back to the door as Mr. Levin, Ms. Hecksher, and Mr. Ippolito walked briskly away, disappearing around the corner.

When Mr. Levin called the break, Kyle headed straight for the empty hallway leading to the football field, wanting some time alone with his throbbing ankle. Next to a row of lockers, he could see through a window to the field. The varsity squad was out there practicing, and the new guy at wide receiver—Kyle's old position—was pretty good. Pete Newman, it looked like.

He turned as he heard footsteps pounding on the tile floor.

"Oh!" Casey Chang stopped short as she came into view, surprised to see him. "I'm sorry. I . . . I just . . . want to get to my locker . . . I'm sorry . . . "

"Hi, Sorry," Kyle said, "I'm Grateful." His dad's favorite stupid joke.

She walked swiftly past him, her hair falling in front of her eyes, and opened her locker. "You were good today."

"Right," Kyle said, trying to sound grateful. "Thanks."

"You were," Casey insisted.

Kyle shrugged. "Hey. Whatever."

"You don't sound convinced."

Kyle shrugged. "Well . . . I am, I guess. Wait, that doesn't sound right. Maybe not. I don't know. It's just that, well, here's the thing. . . . " He shifted, and a brief stabbing pain shot upward through his leg. "Okay, everybody tells me I'm great. Even when I screw up, sing flat, bump into people, make the wrong entrances, fart onstage—they *still* say I'm great."

"So?" Casey said.

"So . . . I *know* I'm not. I can't be *that* good. It's like when I drop a pass or screw up on the field, my coaches and teammates *tell* me I suck. They really let me have it. But not the Drama Club. And yo, I've been sucking a lot lately."

Casey's locker door thumped shut. She walked over to him tentatively. She was eating something that looked like a candy bar. "They do mean it," she said between chews. "You don't have to be perfect to be good. Everybody makes mistakes and sings out of tune during the early rehearsals. You just need practice. Look, you practice catching and running, right? It's the same with music."

"I know." Kyle rubbed the back of his neck. "But getting a chance to practice isn't that easy. Ms. Gunderson's always too busy. And I don't read music."

"If you want, I can play through the melodies for you on a piano," Casey suggested. "I'm not very good, but I can do that."

"Thanks." Kyle shrugged, not wanting to make a big deal out of this. He shifted uncomfortably, distracted by the shouts from outside. Someone had just made a first down, but it was on a broken-pass play with the downfield receiver in the clear by the goal line. He knew he would never have missed that opportunity. "You're a theater person," he said quietly. "In the theater, how do you know you got it right?"

"What do you mean?" Casey asked.

"Like, in sports for example," Kyle went on, "you *know* what to do. You learn plays, practice them, try them in a game—and then they either work or they don't. And the game just goes on like that until someone wins. With the theater it's different. You sing a song only once in a show, you do each scene once, and that's it. You can't do it over. How do you know if you got it right?"

"Well, I—I guess you never *really* do . . . "

"I thought so." Kyle let out a deep sigh.

"God, this doesn't sound like you," Casey said. "You're always like, Mr. Confident."

"I'm not me. I'm my twin brother, Duke." Kyle smiled. "Yo, do you ever have the feeling you're somewhere you don't belong?"

Casey looked at him cautiously, and he went on.

"Like, something bad happens to you, like your ankle— and suddenly you find a place where you can escape, where you can be someone else? And for a while you think, yo, a new life! Like a fantasy game. And then after a while, things get hard . . . and you realize you're just the same person you always were?" Kyle stopped, laughing at the sound of his own voice. If there was one thing he didn't have, it was a way with words. "God, that's stupid. Forget I said it."

"No, it's not," Casey replied. "I do know how you feel."

"You do? 'Cause to tell the truth, sometimes I feel kind of like a phony around you guys. Not always. Just like when I can't tell my right leg from my left in a dance. Have you ever felt that way? Like a phony and you just want to run away?"

He glanced at her, but she was reaching into her shoulder bag, pulling out a cell phone. "It's Charles," she said. "We're supposed to come back. See you there."

Funny. He hadn't heard the phone ring or buzz or anything.

She turned and ran around the corner, back toward the auditorium. But not before he got a good look at her face. She was crying.

11

From: <dramakween312@rport.li.com>
To: <rkolodzny@yaleuniversity.edu>
Subject: ur offline AGAIN so im sending this e-mail
cuz i miss u!!!
September 22, 2:02 A.M.

rachel!
you must be studying too much or making the beast
with two backs with some hot yalie if there is such
a thing. i can't wait for you to get online or turn on
ur cell cuz i HAFF to tawk. im kinda buzzing. u know
me at 2 in the morning. weeeee. don't joke, i will
not have a blood test hahaha.

ok, update. week 1, *Godspell* rehearsals.

what a difference a small cast makes. no blood
and guts like *sweeney todd*. no cast of thousands

like *carousel.* no animals peeing on stage, like *annie.*
10 actors. peace, love, and the gospels. so:

mr. ippolito is in the doghouse for trying to get
us a rusty metal fence casey chang suggested.
the early costume designs look like they're on
loan from the big apple circus. today we did half
of act ii, scene 1 in blue light and the other half
in darkness. the turntable began to spin during
"where are you going?" (appropriate title, huh?) and
the choreography still looks a little like spelunkers
finding their way around an unfamiliar cave in the
dark. thats a metaphor. or is it a simile? anyway
charles is a diva, harrison's doing macbeth, reese
is doing "girls gone wild," ethan is comatose, and
corbin is on the verge of a nervous breakdown. i
fight the feeling that I should be up there, acting &
singing. no don't worry i am following yr advice. i
really do like studnt directing.

mostly.

on the bright side, we have casey and kyle. she
knows how to kick ass. and if jesus was as hot as kt,
it's no wonder christianity lasted so long. (forgive
me, it's a JOKE!)

on the dark side, we have reese (and kyle). just
ONCE I would like to see her lift her eyes from
below his waist. and stop telling him he's a GENIUS
every time he blows his nose. and thrusting every
conceivable body part in his general direction.
eventually this treatment will go straight to his head.
or somewhere else. he's only human.

sort of.

o god, rach, is he hot. not that i'm interested.

ok, i'm interested.

if u must know.

ok, he is perfect, rach. i wonder if he's buying what reese is selling.

could he be?

oh god, listen to me, quel bitch. well, I'm sitting here watching old friends reruns, which always put me in a good mood.

friends, and you.

B

"Mood gorning, comrades!" Dashiell said, barging into the costume/prop room. He knew, of course, that Charles preferred that non-Charlettes knock when the door was closed—it was one of the little personal quirks that made the Drama Club the Drama Club. Dashiell, however, had trouble remembering people's little quirks. That was one of his quirks. But it was a Saturday. Aside from Kyle, only the Drama Club officers were here. No teeming multitudes to distract and annoy. Everybody was always a little looser on Saturdays.

Besides, Dashiell had a question for Kyle. And at the moment Kyle stood in the middle of the room, wearing a spandex Superman costume with an oversize S insignia, a red cape, rainbow suspenders, striped bell-bottom pants, and orange clown shoes.

It was a rare high school where the costume designer was ready after one week of rehearsals, but Charles was no ordinary costume designer.

"*Voilà,*" Charles said. "What do you think?"

Kyle glanced dubiously into the mirror. "It's . . . um. Wow. So, this is what I wear in the show? As Jesus?"

"The crown of thorns violates school safety rules, and we eighty-sixed the loincloth for obvious reasons," Charles replied.

Dashiell felt in his pocket for the note he had carefully typed, revised, and finally printed out for Brianna. He had been promising to give it to her for days, but he needed a piece of crucial information from Kyle first. "Hope I'm not interrupting," he said.

Charles glared at him. "You may enter, but kindly leave your calling card with the butler. And tell me what you think of Mr. Touchdown's costume. Give him the reassurance he so richly deserves."

"You last name is *Touchdown?*" Dashiell asked.

"That was a joke, Dashiell," Charles said. "It's Taggart."

"I knew that," Dashiell lied. "And speaking of names, you can call me Dash."

"*No one* calls you Dash," Charles said.

"No one calls you Chuck, because *you* like Charles," Dashiell pointed out. "I'm only asking for the same consideration."

"Hey, I'll call you Dash," Kyle said.

"Thank you. Listen, I wanted to ask you something," Dashiell said.

"Uh, Dash? Remember . . . my question?" Charles said. "The *costume?*"

Dashiell shrugged. "It looks great—and that's coming

from a guy who prefers Marvel over DC. It evokes that postmodern iconic kind of mental paradigm shift."

"That's what we like about Dashiell—he's a human SAT vocabulary builder," Charles said.

"I don't know, guys . . . ." Kyle fidgeted in front of the mirror. "I wore something like this on Halloween, about ten years ago."

"Honey, people *wore* stuff like this in the seventies," Charles said. "Well, maybe not the clown shoes or the cape. But it's not only that. The design spirit comes from ancient religious pageants. They were all about goofy costumes and pratfalls. That's how they told stories to the masses. Through colorful mythic costumes and exaggeration."

"Well, I'm going to be toast with my teammates," Kyle said. "They'll never let me live this down."

"Um, excuse me—shoulder pads, masks, and padded thighs?" Charles said. "These are not ridiculous?"

Kyle let out a howl of laughter. "Okay, good point. See? I spend my life looking stupid. What do you two guys know about being ridiculed?"

"Well, is it time for confessions?" Dashiell said, "I'm six feet six, maybe one twenty-five when wet. I'm atrocious at sports, but that's all everyone ever asks me about—do you play basketball? They act like I'm a mutant when I say no. My favorite part of gym? Sitting in the stands and reading *Ender's Game*."

"I'm a charter member of the club, too," Charles said with a sigh. "My mom believed in fat kids and so created me in that image, which I have been trying to shake for years. Mom also managed the church thrift shop. So I got plenty of clothes—miraculously preserved from the 1980s. How do clothes stay perfect for twenty years? I figured they came from kids who had died. Maybe from being too fat. Their parents kept the clothes in drawers, weeping and caressing the material. Getting dressed was a grim experience. Going to school was an exercise in embarrassment. Nobody asked *me* if I played basketball. I was the last one picked for team sports in gym. The opposite team would laugh and say 'You got *Scopetta!*' like it was a disease."

"You are kind of contagious," Dashiell pointed out. "I mean, in a good way. Hence, the Charlettes."

Charles shot him a glare then turned back to Kyle. "Look, Kyle," he went on, "the costume is great. You're an actor now. If you were in *Into the Woods*, you would wear tights. People don't care. Not the audience, and especially not the Drama Club."

Dashiell smiled. "The Drama Club—geeks and freaks welcome."

"People appreciate me here," Charles said. "That's all I want in life. This is the best place for people who are different."

Kyle looked at them both in amazement. "Wow, I never had *any* of the problems you guys had."

"We suspected that," Charles said drily. "Look at it this way, Kyle, the fact that you've never been different—that's what makes you different. Don't you see? Now, for that nugget of wisdom, leave a check with my secretary. And resist the temptation to wear your costume home."

Kyle grinned. "Up, up, and away," he said, heading for the door.

"Wait!" Dashiell said. All this talk had distracted him from his goal—information gathering about Brianna. More specifically, Brianna's availability relative to Kyle. If Kyle *wasn't* going with her, then the ball was in play, so to speak. "So, Kyle, um, I was wondering what you were doing on Friday night?"

The question hung in the air. Both Kyle and Charles looked at him oddly.

"Dashiell?" Charles said. "Are you asking Kyle on a date?"

"*Whaaaat*? NO! I mean, no way! I mean, I wasn't asking for . . . I just meant . . . I wanted to know this info for the sake of someone else . . . a girl!"

"Ohhh," Kyle said with a smile. "Who wants to know? Reese? Brianna?"

"I'm not supposed to say," Dashiell said. Actually, Kyle's response had told him exactly what he needed to know. If Kyle was asking that question about Brianna, then logically, that suggested he *wasn't* going out with her.

"Actually, someone else I know would like the same information." Charles laughed. "I guess we've had a few inquiries."

"Just hanging with my football buds that night." Kyle shrugged. "Yo, this may be my last chance. They won't want to know me after they see this costume. No offense, Charles. I *am* cool with the costume. You did a good job. But I know these dudes."

"Well, good luck and godspeed," Dashiell said, quickly backing out of the room.

Mission Possible was under way.

Day by Day

October 1

12

dramakween: i cant beleive ur awake this early on a mondy, rachel. im not humen yet. i didn't sleep last nigt.

YaLeBiRd: party girl.

dramakween: lol. no, homeework. ap world is a bithc. so's calc. im tierd

YaLeBiRd: ur speling sux. how'd u make it thru?

dramakween: fear and whatever else I can find, lets talk about good news.

dramakween: like 2nd week of reheaarsal. it was sooooo good. like a birth. we nailed the openng scene.

dramakween: ha, that IS a birth sene. the disiples hearing the call, coming together from diff walks of life.

dramakween: then harrisn baptiszing kyle in teh big public fountan. kyle singing god save the people.

kyle becoming the leader and teacher. god, when he sings "prepare ye," you wanto just hop on the stage. u know hes really smart, rach. and funny.

YaLeBiRd: *have you slept w him yet? :/*

dramakween: no comment.

YaLeBiRd: *. . . . .*

dramakween: no.

YaLeBiRd: *damn.*

dramakween: mmmm

YaLeBiRd: *how are the problem children?*

dramakween: everyone's beter. harrison is so mgnetic on stage! lori & corbn are frinds cuz he make her laugh by doing fake opera voices. jamil, lynette, becky, & aisha are singing & dancing great.

dramakween: we almost got rid of ethan, but casey rembered his "smith and smythe" stand-up act with corbin.

dramakween: she put thm in a cornner & had them do improv. they playd two drunkerds trying to seduce a curtain . . .

dramakween: a surfer dude robing a bank, etc. ect. i almost peed, I lauged so hard. so ethan's out of the doghous and we're puting teh improvs in the show.

YaLeBiRd: *coolio. & dashiell? my main man?*

dramakween: weird. hes ben promisng 2 giv me this note, 4 like ever? finaly did it on Firday. i thoght it was like a poem or luv note. he just wnts me to look at the new comuputer cue sheet.

YaLeBiRd: *uh-huh, yeah, I believe that.*

YaLeBiRd: *hey, you still bummed abut not acting?*
dramakween: a little. but not realy. dam im so tired. my fingers r made of wwood. i wish u were here.
YaLeBiRd: *you wish kt were there* ☺
dramakween: . . . sigh . . . true dat.

Dashiell carefully lit each candle. Vanilla/jasmine, for Fantasies. Cedar/spruce/rosemary, for Love. Moroccan rose/chamomile, for Positive Energy. Awesome.

Pit check.

He sniffed his armpits. Sweet. As well they should be. He had deodorized them in the morning, then again after gym, and just before this study period. Still, you never knew for sure. There were rules of self-preservation, hardwired from the dawn of time. You can't blink when you hammer your own nail. You can't sneeze with your eyes open. You can't smell your own bad breath. Maybe smelling your own BO was part of that, too.

He pulled a bottle of Old Spice from his desk drawer. He had already put some behind his ears, but a little under each pit wouldn't hurt. Dab, dab. *Voilà.*

Okay, three minutes to go.

Dashiell flicked on his iPod docking system—Jeff Buckley, "Hallelujah," soft and low!—and shut the lights. The projection room went dark, save for the dancing shadows on the walls made by the candlelight against the audiovisual equipment.

Perfect.

It was crucial not to let this seem too calculated. *Oh, just listening to my playlist. Picked up the candles during lunch and wanted to try them. Just a way to make the projection room feel like my bedroom.*

No. Not bedroom!

Like my own personal space.

He sat by his console screen and reviewed the social flowchart—every scenario that could possibly happen this evening neatly laid out on pathways, with alternate strategies for each. When he was satisfied he had it memorized, he exited the document, leaving only the lighting-cue spreadsheet on screen. He would appear to be busy—he was always busy—and when the door opened, he would swivel casually on his wheeled office chair. *Oh, we had a meeting? I almost forgot....*

The knock on the door nearly made him jump. "Come in!" he squeaked.

The door opened, letting in a column of harsh fluorescent light. "Dashiell?" a familiar voice called out.

"Oh, we had a—?" He swiveled toward the door a bit too fast. His size 14EE New Balance 991s caught a dangling ethernet cable. It was attached to a router, which slid inexorably to the edge of the table.

Dashiell lurched forward. His chair reacted with an equal and opposite force, rolling backward and throwing him to the floor.

"Ahhhh!" He reached out desperately. The router plopped firmly into the palm of his right hand—just as Brianna entered the room.

"What the—?" she said.

"Alas, poor Netgear," Dashiell said meekly, lifting the router to eye level. "I knew him, Brianna."

Brianna stared at him in utter bafflement.

"*Hamlet*," Dashiell explained.

"Um, Dashiell?" she said, her eyes now taking in the whole room. "What a piece of work is this?"

What a piece of work. That was another saying from *Hamlet*. This was Brianna's game. He should have anticipated it. Three seconds into the meeting, and already two things that were *not* on the flowchart. "All the world's a stage?" he offered.

Brianna burst out laughing. "This room appears no other thing to me than a foul and pestilent congregation of vapors."

Ouch. "Don't you like the scents?"

"The candles are nice, but I think someone spilled aftershave on the floor." Brianna sat in the vinyl cushioned chair, whose surface Dashiell had carefully repaired with duct tape. She leaned forward. "Dashiell? Are you wearing *hair gel*?"

"A little. And it's Dash." Dashiell smiled and opened a file cabinet drawer, where he had stored a wooden cutting board that contained a chunk of Kraft Cracker Barrel circled impeccably with Ritz crackers. "Would you like some? I have some Vitamin Water in here, too."

Brianna gave him a funny look. "Sure. And then we'll talk about the problems with password protection for the lighting cues?"

"What?" Dashiell said. *Knife*. He had forgotten a knife! How was he going to cut the cheese?

"Wasn't that the reason for this meeting?" Brianna asked.

"Oh. Right . . ." Dashiell pulled open the pencil drawer

of his desk and rummaged around until he found a plastic knife. It still had a little caked residue from last Tuesday's banana-walnut muffin on it, so he wiped it clean with the corner of his shirt. Cutting Brianna and himself each a generous hunk of cheddar, he put them on Ritz crackers and handed her the bigger one. "Better to talk on a full stomach."

"Uh, thanks."

"Vitamin Water? I have Energy and Balance."

"I'm okay."

As Dashiell scarfed down his snack, he noticed she was just holding hers with a strangely reluctant expression. Duh. A napkin. He reached into the drawer and pulled out a stack of napkins he had hoarded from the deli. The top one had some kind of stain on it, so he threw it out and gave her the next one. Then he made sure to carefully swallow before he spoke. "So, the show is going pretty well, huh? That Kyle is an awesome singer."

"Very talented," Brianna said.

"Popular, too. He's going out with his football cronies on Friday, I hear."

"I wouldn't know. I'm busy. Friday's unfortunately a homework night."

Okay. Her story jibed with Kyle's. Just double-checking. That was the response he expected. The branch of the flow-chart he had outlined in gold. Now for the payoff pitch. He would angle for the *next* Friday, October 11.

Despite himself, Dashiell began to shake. "W-well, I was w-wondering—"

"Actually, I hope he doesn't have a date with his buds

a week from Friday," Brianna interrupted, "because that means he couldn't come to my party on that night. Which everyone is invited to."

"P-party?" Dashiell said. "Friday? The eleventh?"

"Oops, study hall's almost half over. Got to go." Brianna rose from the chair, smiling. "You'll be there, won't you? Or did you have other plans?"

"No!" Dashiell nearly shouted. "I mean, I'll check. If I don't, I'll come."

Kyle groaned. "He *didn't*."

"He did," Brianna replied, putting a dollar into the juice machine. As the bill buzzed into the slot, she looked behind her. The crowd in the cafeteria was sparse, most of the kids sitting over by the window. Mr. Mansfield, the eighth-period study hall teacher, looked at her sternly and put his fingers to his lips. "I don't know why I'm telling you this," Brianna whispered to Kyle. "You have to keep absolutely quiet about it. He is the sweetest guy."

"He tried to seduce you with cheddar cheese and Ritz crackers?" Kyle said. "I should have a talk with him."

"About what?"

"I'd use Brie."

"Shhhh," said Mr. Mansfield.

Brianna grabbed her Snapple from the chute, took Kyle by the arm, and dragged him into the hallway. "I adore Dashiell. He's smart and kind and the loyalest friend. I just had to tell someone. And you were in the hallway. I thought I could trust you. If you mention a word of it to those Cro-Magnons you play football with—"

"Don't worry," Kyle said with a smile. "I'm not the kind of guy who gets off on dissing others. Dash is safe. Seriously, I was just like him when I was in middle school."

"No, you weren't."

"Okay, not as smart, but I didn't have a clue about girls. I took Emily Fenwick to the diner but forgot to bring money. So I asked *her* to pay. She came up with two dollars and forty-one cents. I sat there, like, duh. Somehow Harrison's dad figured this out and felt sorry for us. He let us have two grilled cheese sandwiches and two waters without paying. I felt like crap eating that grilled cheese. I didn't say a word to Emily. We practically ran out after the last bite. That weekend I saw Niko, the waiter, in town, and he thanked me for the tip—only I hadn't left one! It turns out Mr. Michaels slipped a few bills onto our table to cover us."

Brianna laughed. "Did you ever pay back Mr. Michaels?"

"I tried. He'd always point to the calculator and say, 'Eenterest, I chhhaff to charge eenterest!' Then he'd burst out laughing and never do anything about it."

This didn't surprise Brianna one bit. Even in middle school, Kyle had been getting away with murder. "Well, at least Dashiell was more thoughtful than that. He bought the food and the candles in advance. Except one of the candles smelled like Old Spice. Or maybe that was him."

"So what did you do?" Kyle asked. "Did you tell him off?"

"I thanked him. I told him the projection room looked cool. I think he wanted to ask me out for Friday after next, so I invited him to the party, which was a convenient way to get out of that. Then I told him the truth—it was study period and I had to do homework. He was very sweet. He smiled and opened the door for me."

"But you lied," Kyle said. "You're not doing homework."

Brianna elbowed him. "I have still have seven minutes left. I do take study hall seriously, you know. And so should you. Rehearsals kill your homework time. Oh, don't you forget: cast party on Friday, the eleventh. My house. Be there."

"Yes'm," Kyle said. "Hey, if I sit with you and study right now, will your brains rub off on me?"

"That is a disgusting image."

They walked back into the cafeteria and took seats at a table, opposite each other. Brianna briskly opened her math textbook and notebook, both of which she'd bookmarked to the right page. She ignored Kyle as best as she could. As it was, she had enough homework to keep her going till two A.M. Again.

Her cell phone vibrated in her pack, and she glanced down at the screen. It was Harrison. She would pick up the call later.

"Hey, Brianna?" Kyle whispered.

"Hmm?"

"You gave Dash respect. I like that. You were good to him."

Brianna smiled. "I'm a good respect giver."

"Yeah, to me, too," Kyle said.

Now she had to look up. "What did I do?"

"Nothing." Kyle shrugged. "No, something. You forced me to audition. Well, that's not respect, really. But you, like, *noticed* my singing. And you didn't say it sucked dead yaks. Like most of the football dudes in the locker room."

"You sing in the locker room?"

"Sometimes. Until they squirt me with Gatorade. Well, they don't do that anymore because I'm never *in* the locker room—which is kind of a problem, being that this was the season I was supposed to break four records. And maybe help us get into the championship for the first time in thirty years. Everybody's pissed—especially the coach. But hey, now I get to be like a star. So, you know . . . um, thanks."

That was the nicest thing anyone had said to her in days. "That's sweet, Kyle . . . ."

He leaned closer. "Hey. I wanted to ask you—"

"Shhhhhh!" said Mr. Mansfield.

Kyle pulled back and began digging in his backpack for his homework books. Brianna wasn't sure, but his face looked as heated as hers felt.

13

"HEY, CASEY."

"*Brianna*? It's really late. What time is it? Are you okay?"

"Sorry. Were you sleeping?"

"Yes. I mean, no. I mean, it's okay, don't worry. What's up?"

"He said he wanted to ask me something. In study hall. Mr. Mansfield shut him up, and then he kind of forgot about it."

"Who?"

"I can't stop thinking about it."

"Brianna, you're not making any sense. Who wanted to ask you what?"

"Kyle."

"*Kyle?*"

"I think he likes me."

"*What?*"

"You heard me."

"Um, well, that's great! I mean, isn't it?"

"I wish I knew what he wanted to say."

"Wow, Brianna, this doesn't sound like you."

"I know, I know. Can you believe it? I can't believe it. It's only a guy. I'm sorry, Casey. Welcome to my secret life as a cheesy soap opera. What time is it?"

"Almost three o'clock."

"I'm wired. Too much homework. I have to get some sleep. Casey?"

"What?"

"It's going to be okay, right?"

"*Brianna?* Um, wow, yeah. Sure. Definitely. Oh God, I get insomnia, too, and it's like the world is going to end. But then the next day you feel fine. And don't worry about Kyle, okay? He's probably drooling over you in his dreams, as we speak."

"Thanks. Sorry about this, Case."

"No, it's okay. That's what friends are for."

"Uh-oh . . ."

"What?"

"I hear a song coming on . . ."

"You are crazy."

"No. Yes. Maybe. Night, Casey."

"Night, Brianna."

14

From: <kylester41@rport.li.com>
To: <maddogpigskinpete@rport.li.com>
Subject: Re: is benny deaf?
October 5, 5:48 P.M.

yo petey, dont be so mad at benny hes cool. i saw you guys through the window so I know what you're talking about. look, you gotta really yell to the qb when ur in the clear like CLEEEEER!!! benny will really hear that ee sound, you know? anyway i'll be joining u guys soon coz i really suck at this. i thought it was cool but this week was bad. i tried to sing this important song that happens during the crusifiction (sp?) scene, yes i know it sounds stupid, but i can't get it and don't tell me u can help me with that voice like a cross between a frog and a walrus. hey, its my funeral. i'm gonna work on my car. thatll make me feel better. come help. bring a new alternater ha ha ha.

K

"Lori has the *flu?*" Casey said softly into her cell-phone headset, hoping none of the teachers would see her using it. The last bell had just rung, and she was making her way through the school's crowded hallways. "Wow. She didn't look sick yesterday."

"She didn't look sick this morning in math, either," Harrison's voice replied. "She called me during eighth period. It must have happened suddenly. She says she'll be back tomorrow."

Casey rounded the corner, heading toward the auditorium. She took the pretzel from a bag she had just bought from the snack machine. The wall of photos loomed up on her right—as always, surrounded by a group of students. One of them had "found" herself among the images. You could always tell. "With the *flu?* How can Lori be so sure?"

"Good question," Harrison replied. "Can we set up an emergency audition if we have to?"

"Of course. I'll call a meeting."

"How soon can you get here?"

"I'm in the lobby. But there are, like, seven hundred parents. See you as soon as I can."

She flipped the phone shut, zigzagging through the

lobby. Today was make-up day for moms and dads who hadn't been able to attend the recent parent-teacher conferences. From the looks of it, the conferences must have been a bust. It was amazing how much space parents occupied compared to kids. Or maybe they just *enjoyed* standing still in the middle of the hallway, like cows grazing in a field.

As Casey walked, she began riffling through her script. Lori's absence made things complicated. After lunch Mr. Levin had asked Casey if she would run the parable scene while he and Brianna worked on Harrison and Kyle's duet in "All for the Best." Which meant Casey would have to direct *plus* read the missing parts. Naturally, she had spent the entire school day preparing for this fifteen-minute mini-rehearsal. During math class she had memorized Kyle's and Harrison's lines, risking a nuclear attack by Mr. Brotman, who was not very understanding about the Drama Club. Now, after all that, she would have to learn Lori's part as well.

"Excuse me," she said, making her way around the grown-ups clogging the flight paths. "Excuse me!" As she took a detour around a large group discussing SAT scores, she caught a glimpse of a line outside the principal's office.

Lori's mom was there. And she was chatting with her daughter. Who seemed to have made the world's most miraculous instant recovery from the flu.

Casey walked toward her. "Lori?" she called out.

Lori's eyes darted toward Casey. Her smile tightened. She glanced tentatively in the direction of her mom, who was now talking to someone else. With a small but firm gesture, palms down and slicing the air, she made it clear that she couldn't talk.

Casey took another step forward but thought better of it. She turned and hightailed it to the auditorium, nearly colliding with a dad eating Cheetos.

She found Harrison and Charles just inside the door.

"Lori's out there, with her parents," Casey said as the auditorium door closed behind her.

"What?" Harrison said. "I knew they were strict, but they're making her do conferences when she's sick?"

"She doesn't look sick at all," Casey said. "Why would she lie to us?"

"Uh, excuse me, Nancy Drew and Frank Hardy," Charles said. "This is the oldest trick in the book. Lori is keeping her alibi straight."

"Alibi for what?" Casey asked.

"For avoiding the parent-teacher conference," Charles said. "My older brother used to pull this kind of thing. See, if you miss *this* conference, you've got a free pass till next semester—very convenient if your grades happen to be in the toilet. Which you wouldn't think would be the case with Lori, but one never knows, do one? Ergo, Lori wanted to convince her parents she was sick. And she told us the same story because she has Mr. Levin for English and didn't want him to rat her out. But instead of convincing Mom and Pop—which clearly didn't work— she convinced Harrison and Casey."

"That's pretty lame behavior, especially from someone who calls herself a disciple," Harrison said.

Behind them, the door flew open. "Dudes, there are parents *everywhere!*" Kyle cried out, staggering in.

"Love the orange swoop," Charles said, gesturing toward the right side of Kyle's shirt.

"Cheetos," he said, wiping off as much of the Day-Glo stain as he could.

Casey noticed Kyle's fingertips were black. He caught her staring and shrugged. "I was working on my car."

"Ah. The gasoline-Cheeto hybrid," Charles said.

Casey glanced around the auditorium, counting heads. Brianna was tucked into a middle row, working on homework. Good. Maybe she would be able to sleep tonight. "All right, we're all here. Should we get started? Maybe someone can get snacks?"

"Ms. Gunderson has chips, I think," Harrison said.

As they all headed toward the stage, Kyle fell in step with Casey. "You are just the person I wanted to see," he said.

"Me?" She regretted her tone of voice, which sounded a bit too much like the contestant who just won Final *Jeopardy!*

"The solo during the crucifixion scene—'O God, I'm Dying'?" Kyle said. "It *sounds* so easy, but I can't get the notes. I listened to it and listened to it and listened to it, a million times."

Casey nodded. "There are all those weird modulations."

"Modu-what?"

"Key changes. They're hard to hear. You kind of have to do them over and over with a piano."

"Right. So I'm ready to do that with you. Just like you promised me, in the hallway . . ."

She *had* promised. But she never expected him to take her up on it.

"Nobody ever uses those little practice rooms across the hall from the stage," Kyle went on. "They have pianos in them. Maybe we could just sneak away during the rehearsal, just you and me? You could bang it out a few hundred times until I get it into my thick head?"

"Sure," she said, not quite believing that her voice sounded so casual. She could feel her heart doing little cartwheels of joy. "Just let me know when."

Brianna was in the middle of AP world history homework in Row S, simultaneously keeping track of the rehearsal onstage, when a cloud of Old Spice landed in the seat next to her. "Dashiell?" she said.

"Aren't you supposed to be paying attention?" Dashiell asked.

"I'm a slave to multitasking," Brianna said. Up onstage, Casey was showing off the work she had done in the hallway with the rest of the cast. She had vowed to help Kyle nail the soft-shoe number.

"Okay, 'All for the Best,' " Casey called out.

"One, two, three, four!" Ms. Gunderson said, playing the intro.

Brianna crossed her fingers. Kyle and Harrison were holding their rolled-up umbrellas, bouncing to the beat, singing.

"And . . . kickline!" Reese called out.

Harrison kicked right.

And Kyle whacked him in the face with the umbrella.

"*Cut!*" Casey called out.

Brianna winced. Kyle was trying so hard, but he could never get this number right.

She took him in with her eyes. What had he wanted to say to her? It couldn't have been much. Still, the uncertainty stuck in her like an undigested pit. Last night had been hard. Staying awake had been a bitch. She'd snuck some of the caffeine pills her mom had lying around, maybe the equivalent of five cups of coffee, six, she wasn't sure—shouldn't have been that big a deal. But she had done some really stupid things. Like calling Casey. And obsessing over Kyle.

Caffeine gave you jitters. It magnified little things into big deals. Late at night, your left brain was battling with your right brain over the right to sleep. Add caffeine, and your thoughts went haywire. That's what it was. The caffeine.

Casey had been so sweet to her all day, asking how she was feeling, bringing her a cup of coffee at lunch. Like a best friend. Brianna hadn't had a best friend since eighth grade.

"Do you like Monterey jack?" Dashiell asked.

Brianna turned. Dashiell was holding a plastic-wrapped package of cheese in his hand. "Excuse me?"

"I figured since you left your canapé, you didn't like cheddar," Dashiell said. "It does have that sharpness. Walt, the guy at the cheese store, told me this is milder, without sacrificing flavor. He recommended water crackers with it."

"Dashiell, are you trying to feed me cheese *now*?" Brianna asked. "In the middle of the rehearsal?"

Dashiell pulled the package down below the level of the seat backs. "No! I was just wondering. You know. Curious. I was going to bring this home and try it myself."

"Oh. Jack is good. They make it with peppers, too."

"Aha . . ." Dashiell furrowed his brow, as if filing the concept in its proper folder for future reference.

Kyle, who had been talking with Mr. Levin, came bounding up the aisle. He was smiling at her now. What? Was he going to ask now? Why did she care so much?

"Hey," he said, and she noticed his fingers were stained black.

"What happened to your hands?" Brianna asked.

Kyle immediately shoved them behind his back. "I was working on my new car during shop. Vintage '67 Thunderbird. Red."

"Really?" Courtesy of her uncle Paulie, who collected vintage cars to rent to the movie industry, Brianna had actually traveled in one of those. Or maybe a 1969. But close. "Those are so cool. Does it work?"

"Like new," Kyle said. "Well, except some of the floor is missing. But it's a V8. Like driving a spaceship. I was going to tell you about it yesterday in study hall. I wanted to know if you'd like to be the first person to have a ride in it with me. I could drive you home after rehearsal tonight."

A ride in a car—that was it? Not exactly what she'd hoped for, but it might lead to something interesting. "Offer accepted," Brianna said.

"You, too, Dash," Kyle added as he sat in the empty seat on Brianna's right.

Not going to lead anywhere at all, Brianna realized.

Dashiell didn't notice. His attention was riveted on the stage. "Casey is extraordinary," he said.

Brianna took her mind off Kyle and focused. "Don't be fooled by that meek exterior. Casey's a perfect stage manager *and* a natural director."

"You're not so bad either," Kyle said.

"Pshaw," Brianna said.

Dashiell laughed. "That's funny. Pshaw."

"Seriously, Brianna," Kyle said. "You were awesome when you helped me on 'All for the Best.' It made a huge difference."

"Excuse me?" Reese said, managing to appear from nowhere, as always, at just the right time. " 'All for the Best' is a *dance* number, and the choreographer had a hand in it, thank you very much?"

"You're welcome," Kyle said, allowing Reese to do a slow burn before he reached over and bear-hugged her waist.

"*Auuugggh*, your hands are filthy!" Reese said.

Kyle let go, and Reese stood in the aisle with her hands on hips. "What is this, the Brianna Boy-Toy Brigade? We have work to do. Dashiell, Mr. Levin wants to know if you and Kyle can nail the placement for the spots in the crucifixion scene." She gave a little giggle. "Nail? Crucifixion? Oops. Forgive me."

Dashiell rose reluctantly from his seat. "I thought we did that placement already."

"Keeps us off the street, Dash," Kyle said. "I'll do it, as long as I don't have to sing the song."

"Bubbeleh, you can sing the wings off a butterfly," Reese said.

Kyle pinched her on the butt before jogging toward the

stage. Dashiell went in the other direction, toward the projection booth.

"Sexual harassment," Reese murmured. "Do I have a grease stain on my butt?"

Brianna raised an eyebrow. "Yup. I would press charges."

Reese grinned and slid into the seat next to her. "So, I take it our friend Dashiell is after you now?"

Brianna stiffened. "What makes you think that?"

"The Old Spice," Reese said. "Did he offer you chocolate in the projection room?"

"No," Brianna said, not exactly lying. She did *not* want this to turn into gossip.

"Well, that's next," Reese said. "Unless he changes to some other food. I told him girls had mixed feelings about chocolate. Maybe he'll graduate to pâté."

"Thanks for the tip."

"Speaking of tips . . ." Reese leaned in close. "The field is wide open, Brianna. Just wanted to let you know."

"Field?"

"As in, the touchdown pass is in the air? The wide receiver has side-armed the most savage attacker?" Reese gave Brianna a Look of Great Meaning. "Ugh, Brianna, for a smart-ass, you can be so clueless. I'm talking about Kyle. I was hoping . . . but no, to me he's a total lost cause. He treats me like Li'l Sis—and that, as you know, is so not me. So . . . I didn't want you to hold back because of me. I release him. Kyle is yours. If you can hold on to him."

Brianna couldn't help laughing. Reese never did lack a sense of drama. And self-importance. "Oh! Reese, that's so, um, considerate. But I wasn't really thinking about that—"

"Mm-hm," Reese said. "Well, I have a feeling this may

be a limited-time opportunity. If you wait, Brianna, you may have to stand in line . . . "

She was looking at the stage now, where Kyle was standing in a spotlight that was changing from white to blue to red to yellow and back again in rapid succession.

He was not alone. Casey stood next to him, her body turning gently from side to side as she gazed up into his face. He laughed at something she said and then turned toward Dashiell in the booth. "Are we all set, Dash?"

"I think so," Dashiell replied.

"What's next?" Kyle asked Mr. Levin.

Mr. Levin looked at his watch. "Whoa, we ran over. Where does the time go? Okay, cast, time to go home! See you all tomorrow!"

Reese nudged Brianna in the ribs. They both watched as Kyle put his arm around Casey and headed back into the wings.

Casey?

Brianna felt her stomach knot and her teeth clench. "Cute," she said.

"As long as you don't mind," Reese said with a shrug.

"Why would I mind?"

"None of my business." Reese turned away, with a sharp toss of hair over her shoulder. "Just wanted to make sure Casey wasn't screwing up a good friendship."

15

THE FEELING CAME BACK IMMEDIATELY. THE lessons with Mrs. Dunham. Casey's tiny fingers struggling to press the keys. *Here we go / Up a row, / To a birthday party* . . . Casey smiled. There were some things she really did miss.

"Brava, Kara mia!" That was what she always said, Brava. The feminine of bravo. And Kara mia. My dear. Mrs. D took so much joy in their lessons, especially the sight-reading, where they would sit side by side. And after good lessons Casey would get a gold star, until her assignment book was so thick with gold stars that it could barely close. And that last lesson . . . the four-hands version of Beethoven's Fifth, with the sun streaming through the open window . . . and when they finished, Mrs. D said the sky was the limit, but it wasn't, because that was the last day . . .

"Casey?"

She spun around. Kyle was coming through the door with two bottles of water. "Thanks," she said, her voice parched.

"You sound as bad as I feel," Kyle said. He untwisted the top of his bottle and held the water high. "Cheers! Let's hydrate."

"Do you have anything to eat?" Casey asked, suddenly feeling ravenous.

"I'm a football player. I always carry snacks." He pulled a Baby Ruth and a Fast Break out of his backpack and put them on the piano.

Focus. Energize. Casey quickly ate the Fast Break. It soothed going down. She had been eating a lot lately. It was stress. But she would cut down, after today. As she took a long swig of water, she closed her eyes and concentrated on the moment. *Focus on now.* Now was now. Everything else was then. "So, what part is giving you trouble?" she asked. "'All for the Best'?"

Kyle groaned. "The dance number? That is going to suck so bad. I can never get that. But at least that song is easy." He plopped his musical score on the piano. The sheets were dog-eared and marked up with dynamics and directorial suggestions. Quickly he turned toward the back of the score and pointed. "Here. This little part I sing during the crucifixion. I can never do it right."

The line was pretty easy—to play, at least. Mostly quarter notes, dotted quarters, and half notes. Casey could handle that. "Um, let me play it through once first. Then you can sing the second time," she said.

Kyle looked over her shoulder as she played. He smelled good. It wasn't cologne or aftershave, Casey guessed. Probably some kind of soap. A faint scent of the sea. Unconsciously she sat higher on the bench, to be closer to his face, and began playing the intro. "Let's jump right in . . . okay, two, three, four . . . *now!*"

"'Oh, God, I'm dying . . .'" Kyle sang.

"Perfect—keep going!" So far, so good. But he had to sing the same line in a couple of different keys. Together they counted through the rests. "And . . . *now!*"

"'Oh, God, I'm dyiiiing . . .'" Kyle sang.

"Almost," she said, stopping the music. "Very close. Let's try that again."

He was even further off the next time.

Casey pounded on the E, F, and F, singing three sentences to the tune: "Dy-ing! A-little-higher! Here-are-the-notes!"

"I *am* dying," Kyle said, flattening himself against the practice room wall.

She'd been too harsh. She was alienating him. "Sorry!" she said.

"Yeah, I know," Kyle said with a crooked, goofy grin. "Sorry because the Drama Club cast me. Sorry because you agreed to suffer in this sweaty little box while I mess up the tune. Yo, Stephen Schwartz is spinning in his grave! He's sorry, too."

Casey couldn't tell if he was joking or not. "He's still alive, Kyle."

"He won't be if he hears me." Kyle leaned over the music, staring down the notes. "Come on. Let's do it for Stephen. Time is running out. Fourth down. No punting."

He wasn't joking. Kyle had a neurotic side? It didn't seem possible. But singing brought out that kind of thing. Casey scoured the music, looking for something that would help him hear the tune.

"Your first note?" she said. "It's in the chord just before. You'll hear *this* . . ." She carefully played the chord, then lifted all her fingers except one. "And you'll sing this note. 'O . . . ' et cetera. Got it?"

Kyle looked dubious. "Let's try . . ."

She played—and he came in perfectly. "That's it," Casey said.

"Whoa, that's *it*?" She felt his arms around her, and she quickly turned—in time for him to sweep her up in a big bear hug. "I got it? *I got it*?"

Casey felt her feet leave the ground. She held him tight as he swung her around the tiny space, and she buried her face in the folds of his shirt and took a deep breath. She realized it wasn't soap. It was just him.

He let her down at the piano bench, and she unwrapped her arms. Over his shoulder she could see a slight movement in the thick window of the practice room door. The window was small, just big enough for a face.

Brianna's.

Casey leaped from the bench and opened the door. "Did you hear Kyle? He was—"

"I don't want to interrupt anything," Brianna said.

"You're not!" Casey replied.

Brianna smiled tightly. "No. Go ahead, Casey. You just pretend I'm not here."

"We're just running a song," Casey said.

"Join the party!" Kyle added.

"I'm not in a party mood. Really. Keep going." Brianna backed away, pantomiming a phone. "I'll call— "

"But—" Before Casey could say another word, Brianna was gone.

Casey felt her adrenaline flow out of her body and down through her toes into the carpet.

Brianna was mad.

But *how* could she be mad? Did she honestly think . . . Casey and Kyle? Okay, the hug must have looked a little cozy. But even if it *were* possible—about as likely as the sun and moon deciding to switch places—did she really think Casey would try to steal him away in a *practice room?*

"That was weird," Kyle said, reaching over to flip the song back to the beginning. "Oh, well, let's do it again."

Casey forced herself to concentrate on the notes. It was ridiculous. She and Brianna were *not* in competition. The idea was absurd. She played through the song and then hit his chord. Kyle got his entrance perfectly and whooped with delight. But as she continued to the next page, he suddenly slapped his forehead. "Oh, damn."

Casey stopped. "What?"

"I promised Brianna a ride home," Kyle said. *"That's why she was acting so strange."*

"Uh-oh." Casey went out the room and ran out into the hallway. The practice rooms were in the music section, across the hall from the side door of the auditorium. She threw the door open and looked inside, but only Mr. Levin and Mr. Ippolito were there. Mr. Ippolito was grinning.

Mr. Levin gave her a thumbs-up. "Guess what? Mr.

Ippolito straightened things out. We're getting a brand-new Cyclone fence, compliments of the PTA!"

"Great!" Casey said with as much enthusiasm as she could muster. "Um, have you two seen Brianna?"

"She left a few minutes ago," Mr. Levin replied. "She was looking for Kyle."

"Thanks."

Casey shut the door and backed into the hallway, where Kyle was waiting. "I am a real ass," he said.

"Do you think Brianna's mad at *me*?" Casey asked. "Maybe she thinks . . . you and me . . . ?"

"Brianna is cooler than that," Kyle said with a reassuring kind of chuckle, although the statement did not make Casey feel particularly tingly inside. "Don't worry, Casey. It's totally my fault. A broken promise to ride in a T-Bird? Yo, that's tough to recover from. I'll call her."

"You will?"

"Yup." Kyle looked at his watch. "Well, as long as the passenger seat's empty . . . you want a ride?"

It was getting dark out, and tonight her mom was working night shift at the hospital. Casey had her usual qualms about getting into a car. Then again, the temperature had dropped sharply today, and she hadn't been looking forward to the lonely walk home.

He held out his arm. With a smile, Casey took it.

And as they walked toward the door, Kyle pressing her close to his side, she had the funniest feeling. It hit her hard, sort of like discovering, after all these years, that the world actually is banana-shaped.

Was Brianna picking up something that Casey wasn't? Was *Kyle* actually interested in . . .

No. It wasn't possible. Not Kyle. Not her.

Don't flatter yourself, Chang.

As he opened the door, his eyes were wide and unflinching. "You will love this," he said.

She let in the thought—just for the briefest of moments, she entertained the idea that he might, just might be attracted to her.

And then she let it go.

Some things were just too wild to be true. The world was round. The sun and the moon were where they always were. That's all there was to it.

16

From: <dramakween312@rport.li.com>
To: <rkolodzny@yaleuniversity.edu>
Subject: i can't sleep
October 6, 3:07 A.M.

rachel

weeee yes it's 3 a.m. and i am buzzing buzzing buzzing but thinking clearly and i made the BIG mistake of calling someone last night & waking them up & don't want to do the same to you (someone i actually LOVE and RESPECT) so im sending this e-mail hope you don't mind. you were right, rachel. about kt. i have turned into the kind of girl i hate and don't say i told you so, i can't take that. i shouldn't care about this, ok he's a good singer and oh is he HOTT but lets face it he's flaky and his fingers are full of grease plus his best friends act like they just emerged from caves. so now he and casey are hooking up in the practice rooms and i want to scream. how do i know they were hooking up? because that's what practice rooms are for, i know it from, um, personal experience and admit it, you do too as i recall from those steamy windows when you and bruce greenberg were "practicing." ok, so kt likes cc. why shouldn't he? what's the big deal? she tries hard, she's smart, and she can play piano for him. okay, i can play piano too but he didn't ask me, besides i'm a lousy sight-reader, but hey, if she wants to show off, that's her choice. what do i care? what bothers me isn't so much THAT. it's the shape-shifting. pretending to be your best friend and then stabbing you in the back. i never trusted her. she sings but doesn't sing, she's shy but bosses people around, she falls apart at a criticism but runs rehearsals. what bothers me is that just when you think you know her she slips through your hands like water. who is she? she is hiding something, i can feel it.

ok, don't yell at me but i searched google for "casey chang" westfield connecticut & came up with nothing. just plain "casey chang"? nada. blog search, myspace, facebook, xanga, waybackmachine, big fat zeroes. well, it's not totally true. i did find a chang in a cast list for fiddler on the roof at westfield high, with a different first name, not casey. but chang is like smith, so that's not too shocking. no one ever friended her? mentioned her? this is the girl kyle is hot for—a person with no identity?

i should call alex duboff, that's it. she knows him. he'd know. the only problem is, i'd have to talk to alex duboff.

oh god, i can't even read this. i feel like a stalker.

burn this e-mail.

B

"Excellent!" Ms. Gunderson called out to Lori, who had not only made a full recovery from the flu but was sounding more and more magnificent. "Take a rest, sweetie. You deserve it."

As Lori left the stage, Casey unwrapped a big, cakey brownie and took a big bite. Thank God for the Bayview Avenue food truck, this week's best discovery. It had taken until October 9, but better late than never. She glanced at her schedule sheet. A big purple-red blotch covered the second act, the remnant of a spilled Diet Coke. It obliterated a line or two, but she had memorized most of this by now. Swallowing carefully, she called out, "Um, places for 'All Good Gifts'!"

Kyle looked up from his stretching exercises on the stage. "Okay, chief!"

Casey smiled at him and immediately turned away. Her first instinct was to check for Brianna. Brianna hadn't said a word to her since last week. She hadn't been at her locker lately, and during the rehearsals she was always either studying the script or looking in the other direction whenever Casey passed by.

A hundred times Casey had meant to talk to her, but the day-to-day schedule was grueling for the stage manager. The few times she had started to approach Brianna, she'd gotten cold feet.

Kyle didn't seem to have a clue about the friction he was causing. Or maybe he did, but he just didn't care. Either way, she envied him. Of course, envy was the least complicated of the feelings she had for Kyle. Surprisingly, the ride home had been fun, rolling down the roof and singing at the top of their lungs. It hadn't gone any further than that, but she hadn't expected it to, really.

Surely she must have come to her senses by now. Just a moment's thought about the absurdity of it all . . . *Hmmm, let's see: Kyle and the fat, dumpy, insecure girl . . . or Kyle and the talented, beautiful, brilliant one who discovered his talent and changed his life?*

Tough call.

Casey took another bite.

"A styrachosaurus," Charles said, staring over her shoulder.

"Nope, just a brownie," Casey said.

Charles gave her a look. "That shape on your cue sheet. It's like a Rorschach test, right? Identify the blot? Well, I see a styrachosaurus. You know, the one with all those horns around its crown, the most colorful and stylish of reptiles? The Tommy Hilfiger of the Mesozoic age?"

Casey laughed, pulling flecks of brownie up into her nasal passages. She began coughing violently.

Charles patted her on the back. "Don't do this to me, Casey, I've seen all those posters for the Heimlich maneuver, but I can't remember how to do it!"

"Don't—" *Cough, cough.* "Make me—" *Cough.* "Laugh!"

"QUIET BACKSTAGE!" Brianna's voice shouted from the auditorium.

"Shh, Miss Diva is in a bad mood," Charles whispered, ushering Casey farther into the wings.

Some of the Charlettes, seeing Casey's condition, dragged a chair over so she could sit. Vijay brought her some bottled water. She sipped it carefully, clearing her throat as quietly as possible, and angling her chair so she could see the stage.

Jamil was singing "All Good Gifts," one of her favorites. He was a freshman, and his voice hadn't changed yet. It had a pure, sweet quality. He was inexperienced and a little unsure at times, but he was getting stronger by the day.

"Can we stop, please?" Brianna's voice rang out from the house. "Okay, that wasn't bad."

"Can she curb her enthusiasm?" Charles murmured.

Casey stood up and walked to the edge of the stage, glancing at her schedule. "Let's set up for scene—"

"Excuse me." Brianna was walking purposefully down the aisle. "Can we go back to the top of that last song?"

Jamil cocked his head, baffled. "What'd I do?"

"Your tone is good, Jamil. Really, really sweet. I'd just

like to hear it one more time, for pitch." Brianna pointed to her ear. "I think you're singing a teeny bit flat."

Mr. Levin glanced at Ms. Gunderson, who replied with an unreadable look of her own.

"I didn't hear anything wrong," Casey murmured to Charles.

"I could try it again," Jamil said gamely. "No problem."

"Brianna," Mr. Levin said, climbing down from the stage apron, "do you have any *dramatic* notes? Because, in the interest of time, when it comes to musical matters, maybe Ms. Gunderson should make these kinds of calls—"

"Well, it just seemed pretty obvious," Brianna said, lowering her voice. "Besides, this is supposed to be a collaborative effort, right? We all help out. Sometimes we see things others don't. Or hear things."

Ms. Gunderson smiled. "True. Good point. But we're not after perfection, sweetie. The audience isn't that picky about pitch."

"Fine," Brianna said with a shrug. "If you feel you can be proud of that performance, fine." Calmly she turned and walked up the aisle.

"What has gotten into her?" Harrison muttered, jumping off the stage.

Casey followed him. They chased after Brianna and cornered her behind the last row of seats.

"Hello," Brianna said, flashing them a fake smile. "I have to pee. Would you two like to join me?"

"Brianna, what's up?" Casey asked.

"Nothing's up," Brianna said. "I just wasn't aware we were relaxing our standards, okay?"

"What are you talking about?" Harrison asked.

"I guess since it's a small musical, since the *New York Times* won't be there on opening night, it's fine to settle for mediocrity . . ."

"Look, Jamil is a freshman," Harrison said. "He has a beautiful voice that needs a little coaching, and he's very sensitive. He's also getting more and more confident. We want to make him feel at home with us. What's the point in humiliating him?"

"I didn't humiliate him," Brianna said. "I was respectful and professional. Which is more than I can say for some of you. You want to make him comfortable? Then don't lie to him! Don't tell him he's perfect when he's singing flat! You did that to Kyle and now you're doing it to Jamil. You want him to find out the truth from the audience? He has potential, and our job is to help him live up to it."

"Brianna, this isn't such a big deal," Harrison said. "Sometimes it's best to give a performer some time. Let them find their way. It worked with Kyle—his singing improved, right?"

"He didn't find his way all by himself," Brianna said, pointedly looking at Casey. "Now excuse me."

She wiggled between them, toward the door. Harrison began following her, then gave a disgusted wave and came back.

Casey's legs locked.

Brianna *was* mad at her. Those comments had been meant for her. Brianna was pissed about the practice room.

"Don't worry," Harrison said, placing his hand gently on Casey's arm. "She gets like this sometimes. It's usually in the middle of the rehearsal period, when she thinks the show is going to tank. Plus, she's probably frustrated *she* can't be onstage. She'll be okay in a few minutes. She'll apologize to you and Jamil."

"I'm not so sure," Casey said softly.

"I guarantee it," Harrison said, heading back to the stage.

Casey slipped out into the hallway and eyed the girls' room. Brianna was still in there. The thought of confronting her made Casey's stomach hurt. She needed something in it. She darted down the hallway and around the corner to the cafeteria snack machine.

She found a single in her pocket, loaded it into the machine, selected a pack of Sun Chips, then headed back to the auditorium.

As she eyed the girls' room door, which was still shut, she ripped open the chips and popped a few into her mouth. From inside the auditorium, she could hear Mr. Levin's voice booming: "Props? PRO-O-O-OPS!"

That was her. Casey ran. "Sorry!" she called out as she pulled open the auditorium door and hurried toward the stage.

"Casey, where are the canes?" Mr. Levin demanded. "We're running the soft-shoe number, *and we're supposed to have canes today!* Right? These guys have been using umbrellas."

Casey had to think. She had ordered four telescoping vaudeville canes, the kind that look like small wands until you tap them and they spring out to full size. "I'll get them!"

She ran backstage, where the Charlettes had formed a little sewing factory to make the "costume" for a huge beast made of garbage in one of the later scenes. "Guys, where are the canes we ordered?" she asked.

"They sent them to 763 Bayview Avenue, not 163," Vijay said. "So they got sent back."

"I have learned my lesson," Charles said. "I will never allow Vijay of the Woeful Handwriting to fill out a requisition form again!"

"I called them," Vijay said. "They said three to five business days."

Casey stepped back onto the stage and relayed the news to Mr. Levin.

"Three to five days is what they said the first time!" Mr. Levin slapped his hand on the piano, which made a muffled *tonnnnng*. With a disgusted sigh, he turned his back and said, "Let's do it with umbrellas again."

Casey stepped back, nodding, retracing her path, until she bumped into Charles.

"Ooh," said Charles.

"Sorry," said Casey.

"No, that felt good," Charles replied. "Do it again."

"He hates me, too," she said, her back still to him.

"Mr. Levin?" Charles said. "He adores you. He's just a little wigged out. You would be, too, if you had to deal with Miss Diva, fend off the comely Liesl Gunderson, and go home to grade thirty-one reports on *Hamlet*."

Casey turned. Charles was grinning impishly. No one did impish grins better than Charles. Which somehow made her even more depressed.

"Uh-oh, I think we need a change of venue," Charles said, taking her hands and leading her back to the costume/prop room. He shooed away the couple of Charlettes who were inside, sat her down in a puffy leatherette lounger, and shut the door. "There," he said, kneeling beside her. "Now forget the rest of them. Let it all out, babe."

He was reading her mind. He knew she was a mess and he was still totally on her side, and the combination undid her. She couldn't hold it together any longer. Casey took a deep, shuddering breath and gave in.

"I can't do anything right, Charles," she said between sobs. "I can't stop eating, I can't leave the auditorium without something going wrong, and everybody's mad at me!"

"I'm not mad at you," Charles said, handing her a tissue.

"*Yet.* You wait. I'll do something to piss you off, too. I can't help it." Casey wiped her eyes and looked away. "I never should have said yes to this job. I'm not cut out for it. You guys picked the wrong person."

"Oh, dear Lord, Casey, if you quit, this whole clambake will fall apart. Come to your senses, girl. Something's bothering you. Something deeper than this. Talk to Father Charles, my child."

Casey blew her nose. "Father Charles? Am I supposed to confess something?"

"Confess, confide, whatever. I'll take it juicy or dry. Talk to me."

Tap, tap, tap.

Before anyone could respond to the knock, the door swung open and Dashiell poked his head in. "Oh! Sorry. Didn't mean to interrupt. You two just go ahead. I didn't see anything—"

"Come in, Dashiell," Charles said. "What's up?"

"I was going to ask about the blue gels . . ." He gave Casey a curious look. "Are you all right, Case?"

Casey composed herself to answer, but his confused expression just made her cry again.

"Guys, can we please—"

Now Mr. Levin was in the room. He stopped in the middle of his sentence when he saw Casey. The three deep frown lines vanished from his brow, his shoulders loosened, and he let out a sigh. "Um, I think we've all had a long day," he said softly. "I'm calling rehearsal. We could use a break."

"But we have so much to do!" Brianna protested, striding in from the hallway.

"We're in pretty good shape," Mr. Levin said. "And I'm giving you all an assignment. Go home, relax, and do *not* think about *Godspell*. Then dig in tomorrow, and expect a shortish rehearsal on Friday so everyone can rest up for Brianna's party. We are nearly four weeks into rehearsals, but we have a long way to go, and I will not have the disciples hating one another."

"Home, an excellent idea," Charles said. The others began to file out of the auditorium. Charles turned back to Casey. "Take a hot bath, drink some hot cocoa, and call me in the morning."

"You've changed from priest to doctor, I see," Casey answered.

"I'm very versatile, not to mention resilient," he told her. "And so are you. So you'll take my advice?"

Casey gave a last sniffle then smiled. "Yes, Doc. See you tomorrow."

17

"I'LL GET IT!" BRIANNA SAID. FRESHLY SHOWERED and dressed, she ran out of her bedroom. She hoped it wasn't Casey. She couldn't deal with being alone with Casey, first thing on the night of her big Friday party. Okay, at some point she would have to deal with Casey. She was furious at herself for not having the guts to be totally open with Casey, to confront her. If there was one thing Brianna hated more than hypocrites, it was being a hypocrite.

Of course, she wasn't sure if Casey would show. It depended *which* Casey she was tonight. The shy one would be too scared to come, under the circumstances.

The devious, assertive one might just be here to score some more Kyle time.

Brianna swept through the living room toward the front door to answer the bell. *One does not run through the Baronial Suite,* her dad always said, *one sweeps.* It was true. You couldn't help it, in a room with a curving staircase and grand piano, complex Persian rugs, floor-to-ceiling bookshelves stocked with hardcovers that were actually read, a hearth that roared on special occasions like tonight, and her mother's one concession to her dad's strange sense of humor, a fang-toothed collared peccary named George mounted on the mantel. It was an animal something like a boar whose presence made everyone think Brianna's dad was a mighty hunter instead of a business school professor who bought it for seventeen dollars at a run-down antiques shop in Vermont.

Through the window she could see Kyle's T-Bird parked out front, and another car that wasn't familiar. She pulled open the door to see Kyle and Jamil standing there, all washed up and fresh-looking. "Hey, Brianna!" Kyle said, stepping inside.

Nothing in his eyes, in the set of his jaw, his body language, let on that anything was wrong.

Which didn't surprise her. He *wasn't* doing anything wrong. And Brianna wanted to kick herself for it. For not making it clear to him how she felt.

"Make yourself at home," Brianna said, trying not to sound cold.

Her mom came sweeping down the curved staircase, a diaphanous black cape flowing out behind her. Brianna could never master that move without falling on her butt.

But it was no problem for Evangeline Rogere-Glaser, senior manager of the famous Krok Fund ("Because We Serve *and* Return") and owner of the perfect sexy figure and high-cheekbone model's face, both of which had been recently enhanced—er, *rejuvenated*—with utmost surgical taste. "Well, hello, I'm Angie, Brianna's mom!" she called out, her arm extended weightlessly with a line so graceful it seemed like a sin to touch it.

Which Kyle immediately did, grabbing her hand and pumping it like a slot machine. "Kyle Taggart."

"Hello, Mrs. Glaser," said Jamil.

She nodded to Jamil, but her eyes were focused on guess who. "Yes . . . Brianna has told me all about you, Kyle."

"I hope it's all lies!" bellowed Professor Glaser as he rumbled down the stairs in his usual tweed jacket, just a bit small for his expanding belly, and a tie that lay too low on his shirt like one of those helpless hanging squirrels in the Museum of Natural History.

"Me, too," Kyle said with a grin.

"Siobhan is getting Colter ready for bed, so he won't be any trouble," Mrs. Glaser said. "Wish we could stay, but we've got the ballet, and then the board hosts the ballerinas in the Rose Room—all those big fat board members on diets and the tiny dancers eating like hogs. Great fun."

"I match 'em, cheese puff for cheese puff," Mr. Glaser said, behind a theatrically cupped hand.

They swept through the foyer, swept out the door, swept into the car, and swept away down the street. As everyone waved good-bye to them, two more cars pulled up. Casey was in one of them, driven by her mom, who was dressed in what looked like medical scrubs. Brianna locked her face into a smile and waved.

"Time to party!" Kyle shouted.

From the top of the stairs, the wet, freshly combed head of Brianna's five-year-old brother, Colter, popped down between the railing supports. "Time to *poopy!*"

"Pay no attention to the boy behind that banister," Brianna said, picking up a remote on a table just outside the living room and pointing it menacingly toward Colter, who raced upstairs with a squeal of laughter.

Then she pointed the remote at the sound system. Wolfgang Amadeus Mozart politely stopped, and a Jay-Z track made the lampshades vibrate.

"Praying!" Reese blurted out.

Dashiell stopped praying and shook his head. He pointed to his ear.

"Sounds like . . . " Charles said.

Licking his lips with glee, Dashiell pantomimed spooning something out of a tall container.

"Eating!" said Becky.

"Ice cream!" said Jamil.

Dashiell nodded, waved his arms, and continued the mime. *Keep going . . . guess again . . .*

Casey racked her brain. The game was Charades and the topic was Broadway—anything to do with Broadway shows. The music had been turned down, the polished living room surfaces were covered with cartons of mostly eaten take-out Chinese food, Ben & Jerry's ice cream, and empty bottles that would all have to be cleaned out before the Glasers came back. George the collared peccary was wearing a bowler hat and sunglasses, and the antique grandfather clock was about to strike midnight.

She almost hadn't come. But that would have made matters worse. She would have looked guilty, and there was no reason for that. Casey *hadn't* done anything wrong. At some point she would have to talk to Brianna. If not tonight, then soon. She had to keep the channels open. It was all a misunderstanding anyway, and true friendships withstood that.

In the meantime, Casey had put on a good face. It hadn't been easy for an hour or so, and Brianna had barely looked at her. Still, Casey had actually managed to enjoy herself.

What show involved ice cream?

"Ben! Jerry!" shouted Lori.

"Yum! Or . . . yummy?" guessed Aisha.

"Scoop!" shouted Ethan.

"Dessert!" Corbin piped up.

"Sundae!" Kyle said.

Dashiell clapped his hands and pointed at Kyle.

"That's it!" Brianna said. "Sundae. Sundae what?"

Dashiell looked around, thinking. Suddenly he pointed to the stuffed animal on the mantel.

"Pig!" said Charles. "*When Pigs Fly* . . . on Sunday!"

"*When Pigs Fly* was Off-Broadway," Harrison said.

"That's no *pig*," Brianna said indignantly. "George is a collared peccary."

"*Sunday in the Park with George!*" Casey blurted out.

"YES!" Dashiell shouted.

"Go, *Casey!*" Becky shouted.

Casey stood up to take her turn, and Kyle pretended to

pass out. "I give up," he said.

Casey felt herself blushing. She had already gone twice, and maybe her choices—*The Lieutenant of Inishmore* and *A Funny Thing Happened on the Way to the Forum*—had been a little too hard.

"Well, it is kind of late ..." Casey suggested diplomatically.

"How about a different game?" Corbin said.

"Spin the Bottle?" Kyle suggested.

"Now you're talking," Reese piped up.

"How about Truth or Dare?" Brianna blurted out.

Everyone fell silent, mulling it over. Casey felt Brianna's eyes on her. Casey turned to meet her glance, but Brianna looked away. "Let's do that," Brianna said decisively.

"I know a theatrical version," Dashiell said. "All the questions and the dares have to be related to the theater. For example, I say, 'Aisha, what is your deepest fear about doing *Godspell*?' And you either tell the truth or you have to do whatever I dare you to do. Like put a piece of ice down Ethan's back, or kiss George."

"Don't you dare," Aisha said.

"Hostess goes first?" Brianna said sweetly.

"Sure," Dashiell replied. "Now let's form a circle ..."

They all shimmied backward on the living room carpet as Brianna looked slowly around the circle. Her eyes stopped at Casey. "Casey Chang ..."

Casey began to sweat. It was a cool fall night, the fire in the hearth was nearly out, but she felt as if the temperature had risen twenty degrees. She didn't like the look on Brianna's face at all. The truth part of this game was not exactly a place she wanted to go. And her reasons had nothing to do with Brianna or Kyle.

Seal it off. Don't let them come close.

"Not me," Casey said quietly. "Pick someone else."

"No, I want to pick you," Brianna said playfully. "Doesn't everybody want to hear Casey's deepest truth?"

A few voices shouted in agreement, but Casey didn't really hear them. She felt trapped. *Fight or flight.* She gathered her legs under her. "I—I just don't like talking about myself, that's all."

"Everyone opens up to *you*, Casey," Brianna pressed. "Loosen up. Unless you have some big dirty secret—"

"Leave her, Brianna," Kyle chimed in. "It's okay to pass on a turn."

"Then what's the fun?" Brianna said.

She was digging. Why? *Why was she doing this?*

"Darling, not everyone wears their feelings on their sleeves like you and me," Charles said.

"Everyone has secrets," Dashiell added softly. "Stuff that no one is allowed to know."

Secrets.

Mr. Hammond ran the local Catholic charity foundation and enjoyed sailing on the Sound with his two children.... Casey shook away the memories. If you didn't think about the memories, they couldn't hurt you.

Everyone was staring now. The party had changed. The air was different.

Why? What were they all staring at?

Why did Dashiell say that? *Everyone has secrets.* Did they know? Did everyone know? How? It wasn't on the public record, she remembered the report exactly.

Brianna—she knew Alex Duboff. That was it. She must have called him.

Would she do a thing like that? What kind of friend *was* she? What kind of friends were any of them?

Casey stood up, holding herself steady on the edge of an armchair.

"Casey? Are you all right?" Kyle asked. "You look kinda green."

"I'll bet it was the shrimp," Charles said. "Someone smell the shrimp."

"Or the beer," Corbin said.

"Casey?" Brianna was up now, walking closer to her. "Do you want to lie down in my room?"

No. Get out. Now!

"I—I have to go," was all Casey could manage before running for the door and tearing off, blindly into the night.

18

SHE RAN. HER FEET DID THE THINKING, taking her around sharp corners and down placid nighttime streets. Houses blinked and dogs barked and the weary faces of a late-night card game stared at her from a screened-in porch as she passed. She didn't stop until she reached the small park on the corner of Bayview and Merrick.

Unable to think, she slowed her pace and headed toward the duck pond. The park was empty, except for a mass of clothing on a distant bench that was either a sleeping homeless person or two people hooking up. She caught her breath, walking along the edge of the pond and feeling the mist as it blew lightly across the surface of the water. On the opposite side, she could hear a band playing "Oh What a Night" from inside the Olympia Catering House. The place was outlined in Christmas-type lights that reflected in the water, making it look as if there were a happy little duck village under the surface. She wondered how deep the water was. You never could tell. In the dark it was inky black. Under the duck village there could be a population of silent octopi and sharks and a forgotten shipwreck. If she jumped, how far would she go? Would she pass out before hitting bottom, or stand there in ankle-deep water feeling like a lunatic?

The path plunged into darkness just before the hill. Someone had broken three streetlamps, and Casey found the darkness comforting.

She needed to forget the party. Forget what had happened last spring. That's why she and Mom had moved here. The doctors said the adjustment process would take at least a year. Things had been going so well.

Who found out? Maybe Brianna, through Alex Duboff. And maybe Dashiell. He was a Google maniac. But he didn't seem like the type who would go hunting for information on her, and then tell about it.

Unless someone put him up to it.

But why? Why would anyone want to make her miserable? Casey reached into her pack and felt around for something to eat. That was another thing. She was eating all the time. Instead of losing weight, she was getting fat. Again.

Then she heard the footsteps.

Tup-tup-tup-tup-tup.

Heavy. Thick. Male.

In a hurry.

From this angle, she could still see the lump of clothing on the bench, now directly across the pond. If she screamed, they might hear her. But what good would it do?

Cell phone. Where was her cell phone?

She stumbled forward, faster, her pack in front of her. Her hands shook as she reached inside, pushing the mess around—too many things—

Clunk. The phone dropped onto the ground. The footsteps were closer now . . . running.

"Aaaaaaghhhhhhh!" she screamed, turning as a broad silhouette lunged toward her.

"Whoa! Easy!"

She dropped her backpack. The voice was unmistakable. "Kyle?"

He held up his hands. "I come in peace," he said.

"Kyle, you scared the crap out of me."

"I know. Sometimes I scare the crap out of *me*."

"I'm sorry," Casey said, turning away. "Sorry."

"Sorry for what?" he asked. "Hey, are you okay? Want to sit?"

Why was he here? What on earth did he want from her? Had the others followed him?

She pulled back. She didn't want to sit. Or touch. She wanted to move and not stop. "I have to go."

"Me, too. I'm supposed to meet someone in a few minutes, but I can take you home before that if you want. I have my T-Bird." He pointed to the curb.

Casey kept her eyes from his. The last thing she needed was a pitying glance. "You all must think I'm a nutcase."

"Nah. Everyone's mad at Brianna. They think she

pushed you too hard. She feels bad, too. She started crying after you left."

An ambulance whizzed by, siren blaring even though the street was empty. Casey flinched. She hated that sound, even now.

"Want to talk?" Kyle asked.

"It's nothing," Casey replied. "I'll deal with it."

"Cool." Kyle heaved his big shoulders in a friendly way. "Well. Okay then. See you."

Casey watched him walk slowly away, into the halo of the streetlamp. He glanced back over his shoulder, giving her a look that was definitely not pitying but something else . . . what? Protective? Worried? Curious?

That fact that Kyle was *here* began to settle on Casey. He'd followed her. Found her. He could have been with Brianna or his pals or any number of people he hung with on Friday nights. But he was here at the pond, with her, in the mist and muffled din of someone else's celebration.

"Kyle?" she said, her voice brittle in the cooling air. "Why did you really come here?"

He turned to her and shrugged. "No one could figure out why you left. They were all talking about it, but no one was doing anything."

"You were worried—about me?"

He walked toward her. In the reflection of the distant lights his features were shadowed, gray on gray in the fog, but his smile broke through like a crescent moon. "Are we talking? 'Cause you said you didn't want to. Yo, either way is okay. We can hang and *not* talk."

That smell again—salty-sweet, like the ocean. The senses came one at a time with him. Hearing, seeing, smelling.

She felt herself falling toward him and didn't want to stop. "Why . . . would we do that?" she asked. "Not talk?"

Kyle scratched his head. "Guys do it. You could say something important and the other person takes it the wrong way. Or ignores it. Or thinks it's dumb and makes fun of it. So you don't talk. It's safer. That way you don't lose anything."

Lose anything . . .

Casey began walking up the path, toward the darkness and the woods. "Kyle . . . have you ever had some piece of you that you *wanted* to lose?"

He laughed. "Um, that's a hard question. I have to think about that. Have you?"

A reply caught in her throat. Their footsteps echoed over the light-flecked pond, hers sharp and quick, his calmly thumping. They were alone, *she was alone with Kyle Taggart,* and she realized she'd imagined this before, she'd invented this moment in her mind a dozen different times, and not once had she gotten it right. He wasn't doing much, but he was opening something inside her, and she felt herself expanding, like a ripple on the pond. The world began to spin, picking up speed, threatening to sweep her into a limitless void, and the only thing that grounded her was his presence, warm and listening and kind.

"My name isn't Casey." The words were out of her mouth before she could retract them.

"My name isn't Kyle," she heard him say. "It's Roland. Roland Kyle Taggart. But don't tell anyone or I'll have to shoot you."

Shoot me, shoot me quick . . . She was leaving the ground now, whirling, coming apart. She closed her eyes against the dizziness, swallowing against the truth, but it was too late, and there was no going back. Her voice seeped out thickly, like a reopened wound. "I'm Kara. Kara Chang. Does that name ring a bell?"

"Nope."

"That's good . . . I was worried . . . they never released my name, you know . . . "

"Um, what are you talking about?"

Time, too, was spinning now, rewinding, forcing her to see clearly. . . *Late-morning sunlight, dappled through a plane tree. The chatter of squirrels, the screech of a bluebird. Wisteria, Korean spice blossoms. Sight, sound, smell. A perfect spring day.* She looked at him, and if his face had shown shock or ridicule she would have exploded, but it wasn't that way at all. His eyes were inviting, accepting. *Speak.* "I was driving to the 7-Eleven for my mom," she said. "It was April, and I'd had my license for two months. I was good at parking . . . driving in traffic . . . obeying the speed limit, the signs and lights . . . We'd had a huge rainstorm the night before but it was sunny and gorgeous. I must have been doing, like, twenty or twenty-five . . ." Her voice seized up, and she began to shake.

"Come on, Case," Kyle said, "let's sit."

Casey nodded. She steadied herself as they sat on a bench that was way too cold and shrouded in darkness. A shadowy pair of ducks, heads tucked under their wings, floated by like discarded hats.

"I—I wasn't doing anything wrong," she went on. "I knew the corner pretty well. I'd walked by it a hundred times since I was about eight, but still, when you're a kid you don't notice everything. Westfield has a lot of big old maple trees lining the streets, and there was a huge one on the corner, just swooping down. I remember noticing the beautiful light spring green as I passed. I—I didn't see him until I was in the intersection. I couldn't have."

"Him?" Kyle asked.

"It. A car. He was driving pretty fast, but it was a busy street, and he wasn't doing anything wrong. *He* didn't have the stop sign. Anyway, it all happened so fast—I jammed my foot on the brake, but he was already in the intersection, right in front of me, almost as close as you are. I was doing thirty or so, which doesn't feel fast, but it is. I hit him. Right in the side. I must have yanked the steering wheel pretty hard and spun around, because I ended up through the wall of the house across the street and into the living room. I blacked out until they were loading me on the ambulance. That's when I saw the tree . . . and the people . . . and the sun on the other car . . . it was all twisted, and I remember thinking it looked so peaceful, like a sculpture. I knew the people who lived inside the house I'd hit, and I asked if I'd hurt them. The EMT workers told me no, no one was hurt in that family. That was what stuck in my mind, *no one was hurt*, which I took to mean what I wanted it to mean—and then I blacked out again."

"And the people in the other car?"

"I didn't know until my mom told me," Casey said. "After I'd come home. She could barely get the words out. One person was in it. A guy named Kirk Hammond. He'd gone out to buy a birthday present for one of his kids, a

Tickle Me Elmo. The present survived." Casey felt the memory pressing against her chest and throat, pushing upward into her face. "He didn't."

"Oh my God . . . " Kyle muttered.

The tears came down so heavily she couldn't even hold her head up, so she let it drop between her knees as her chest heaved and heaved and heaved. "The newspapers blamed the town," she continued. "The branch on the old maple tree at the corner had split in the storm and drooped down, blocking the stop sign. It should have been removed. Nobody was mad at me. The press, the TV reports, all blamed the town of Westfield. Even his wife told me it wasn't my fault. She *forgave* me. But the look on her face . . . "

Kyle put his arm around her and rocked slowly back and forth.

"I made it to the end of the school year. We were thinking of staying on, but all summer long people were asking about it, my friends, everybody looking at me all funny, like they thought I was going to fall apart—and as the school year got closer I kind of freaked out. My mom started looking for houses in a new place, far away . . . " The spinning had stopped, and she wasn't aware of time anymore. A minute could have been an hour, and it didn't matter because feeling was all, the warmth of Kyle's body as he moved closer and wrapped her in a flannel-warm cloak of comfort and forgiveness. She closed her eyes, feeling weightless, and tasted the shock of his lips. They were soft and sweet and strong, and she kissed him hard, taking from him, feeding a hunger she never knew she'd had. Something coursed through her body, something brighter than light, igniting her as if she had been dead and brought back to life.

Kyle is kissing me.

The thought hung like lights reflected in water, rippling, unreal, burning, blinking in and out of reality. She didn't know herself anymore; she was liquid now, too, melting against his chest. "Kyle . . . I'm . . . "

She cut herself off from saying *sorry*. She wasn't sorry. She knew everything had changed now. Not only between her and Kyle, but between her and everyone else.

"Wow," he whispered.

"Shhhh," she said. The party had ended at Olympia, and the sound of crickets swelled around and beneath them like a blanket.

She let her head rest against his shoulder and felt herself sinking into a kind of peacefulness that seemed utterly new and strange and yet familiar. Maybe for just this moment, everything was all right.

A short time later she felt herself jerking downward and realized she had fallen asleep.

"I'll take you home," Kyle said gently. "You're tired."

"Don't you have to meet someone?" Casey asked.

"No problem, I'll drop you on the way."

She wanted to say yes. She wanted a life of yes with Kyle. But as his eyes caught the streetlamp light and she noticed the pearls of vapor that clung to his hair, she knew what her answer had to be. There could be no car ride after this. Someday she would be comfortable, but not yet. The moment was too fragile, too perfect. "Walk me to the sidewalk," she said with a smile. "Then you go ahead. I hate cars. I want to walk."

He grinned. "You feeling better?"

"Yeah. I really am."

They walked to the curb, and he slipped into his car and waved good-bye. "See you Monday!" he called out.

Casey held her arms out to the side and began to spin. Everything seemed somehow clearer—the edge of the walkway, the corner of the park caretaker's hut, the feathers on the sleeping ducks, the stars. Had she really kissed Kyle? Had this night really happened?

For the first time since the accident she felt things might get better.

Casey took the long way home, around the pond, detouring west along Porterfield Place, all the way to the village green. It was another of her favorite places in Ridgeport, a wide oval of fresh grass with a gazebo in the center and surrounded by wooden benches. Stores lined the streets, mom-and-pop shops alternating with a Starbucks here, a McDonald's there—all of them with hand-painted signs out front. A neon-free zone.

The stores were shuttered, windows deep and black. On one of the park benches a couple was kissing. Feeling like an intruder, she turned to go.

She stopped in her tracks at the sight of the car parked at the curb, empty but familiar.

Her heart in her throat, she turned toward the park bench and walked slowly, silently closer. The two people there were oblivious. A giggle fluttered in the night air, a toss of hair that shone in the pale light of the streetlamp.

Casey shrank into the shadow of a shop entrance. Her eyes locked onto the scene she hoped would somehow magically turn out to be an illusion, a case of mistaken identity. . . .

She heard his name ringing out in a familiar voice, all tinkly and teasing.

For a long moment she stood motionless, feeling the pump of her heart, the air's coolness on her cheeks. She took a deep breath and exhaled, her breath leaving her like a shapeless solid thing, screaming noiselessly into the sky and dissipating among the stars.

She saw Reese's face briefly as it turned upward, then disappeared into the broad profile of Kyle Taggart.

Save the People

November 6

19

"IT IS OKAY, HARALAMBOS. YESTERDAY I THINK we will have good business because of Election Day, but I buy too much food," said Mr. Michaels as he jumped out of the Kostas Korner van, decorated with its famous dancing half men, half goats (which had been scrubbed clear off in certain places where obscene drawings had appeared). He was a man on the go, and he hurried to the back of the van, flinging the doors open. "So . . . I give to your skinny friends."

"Dad," said Harrison, looking over the familiar plastic-covered platters, "this is great. Really. But we have work to do. We can't really stop everything for a big banquet."

This wasn't great. It was wrong. So wrong.

You could cut the air in rehearsals with a cleaver. The

last month had been awful. Dances were lackluster and unimaginative, the singing dull. Casey and Brianna were at each other's throat, and each of them was snippy to everybody else. Dashiell seemed depressed; no one was talking to Reese; Lori seemed nervous; and Charles was on the verge of divorce with the Charlettes. Even Mr. Levin and Ms. Gunderson seemed to be entering a cooling-off period.

Harrison had been hoping for a big rally today.

It was *so* the wrong time, the wrong place, for an unexpected and unwanted shipment of Greek food.

"Banquet? What *banquet*?" Mr. Michaels shrugged, his smile transforming into a look of deep hurt—and Harrison was reminded for the thousandth time where the theatrical gene in his family had come from. "Is just a little moussaka and yogurt and sliced lamb and taramosalata—"

"And baklava," Harrison added, "and custard and honey cakes—*Dad*!"

"What? You don't *like* Kostas Korner food?"

"I love it, you know that! But it's too much. This is a rehearsal, Dad. If they eat all this, it'll turn into nap time!"

"Naps is good!" Mr. Michaels bellowed with laughter as he began stacking platters on his forearms. "Show me where to go."

You couldn't fight it.

A crowd was forming around the van now. "Niiiiice," said a blond girl Harrison vaguely knew.

"It's not for you," Harrison muttered, reaching in reluctantly to grab another platter.

"Plenty for everyone, especially the pretty girls!" Mr. Michaels called over his shoulder, managing to throw a hammy wink to Harrison. "Ooh-la-la! God bless America and don't forget the Greeks!"

"Your dad is cute," the girl said.

"Never saw that man before in my life," Harrison said, thrusting an enormous platter into her arms.

He followed his dad into the auditorium. Mr. Levin was chewing out Vijay about a lost prop. Brianna was buried in her homework. Reese and Kyle were off in the shadows doing God knew what. Casey was running around, replacing masking-tape markers on the stage floor.

Casey straightened up. "We need Jesus and Judas for the tap dance!" she called out, reading from her schedule. "And then we go straight to the junkyard for the crucifixion!"

Harrison could see his dad flinch. This was *not* what they'd taught in the Saint Demetrios Greek Orthodox Church Sunday School. He knew he would hear about this later. *Christos DANCING? Tsk tsk tsk . . . model U.N. . . . politics . . . Intel science . . . THIS is what you should be doing.*

"GOD BLESS AMERICA AND DON'T FORGET THE GREEKS!" Mr. Michaels's booming voice stopped all the other noise.

Harrison cringed. It was his dad's trademark saying, the words hanging in different forms all over the restaurant—stitched into samplers, framed, emblazoned on T-shirts. Everyone in town knew it, but if Harrison heard it one more time, he was going to throw a plate of baklava at the wall.

As his dad headed for the grand piano, Ms. Gunderson

sprinted ahead of him. "Um . . . sorry, no food or drink on the piano, please!" she said, nearly prostrating herself on top of it.

"No problem!" said Mr. Michaels, who then made a great ceremony of lining the edge of the stage with Kostas Korner platters.

"Harrison?" said Mr. Levin, checking his watch. "Is there some occasion?"

"An overflow of food," Harrison replied.

The auditorium fell silent. Reese stared down at the food with a disbelieving sneer. Casey sidled forward distractedly. Brianna looked up and then back down into her homework. Ethan and Corbin came forward, running lines and improvising jokes.

Mr. Michaels glanced around bewilderedly. "Well . . . isn't anybody hungry?"

Mr. Levin hopped down from the stage and smiled graciously. "This is . . . uh, very *generous* of you. Drama Club—how do we show our gratitude?"

Ms. Gunderson began playing "For He's a Jolly Good Fellow," and one by one, everyone joined in. Lori wailed on a high C at the end, which made Mr. Michaels shout "Bravo!" and let out an earsplitting whistle of appreciation.

Soon everyone was thronging around the food. Harrison looked at the clock and watched two hours of rehearsal go up in smoke with just over a week left until opening.

Mr. Michaels threw back his head and laughed, reveling in the adoration.

Harrison ducked into the hallway before he could hear the words *God bless America* . . . one more time.

20

From: <harrison.michaels@rport.li.com>
To: <stavrosdagreek@nyc.cable.net>
Subject: update
November 14, 6:32 P.M.

Dear Stavros,

Tomorrow is DRESS REHEARSAL. Are we ready?
Hell no! Do not try to take the train here (were
you going to?) If you don't hear from me, it means
I'm hiding in humiliation. Thanks for sending the
Shakespearean insults, you may have to use them
on me after this disaster is over, you benighted
addle-pated clotpole.
Till then,
Judas

"Play those keys, honey!" Reese shouted the final spoken line of the song "Turn Back, O Man" in a Mae West accent while flinging her legs over the upright piano, barely missing a square hit on Lori's left temple. Her feet landed on either shoulder of Kyle, who was pantomiming playing the tune.

"Urf," Kyle said, looking up directly into Reese's twilight zone.

"Break!" Mr. Levin called out from the darkness of the house.

Harrison took a deep breath. They were *supposed* to run the play straight through. But what had started as a dress rehearsal had degenerated into Reese Van Cleve Night. She'd been kicking higher, singing louder, and acting broader than everyone else in the cast. They'd had to stop the run-through twice. They hadn't even had a chance to iron out the problems in "All for the Best." Kyle had such a mental block against the choreography. Harrison's shins were covered with scars from his wrong-sided kicks.

"Uh, Reese, where did that move come from?" Brianna asked from the house.

"Like it?" Reese said brightly.

"Uh . . . no, Reese," Mr. Levin said. "Not appropriate, sorry."

Charles, who had emerged from backstage to investigate the commotion, let out a scream. "Oh! We're doing *that* kind of play?"

Reese swung her legs around and jumped off the piano. "The *true* professionals are never understood," she grumbled to Harrison.

"Maybe you should stop practicing your Tony speech and actually interact with the other actors," Harrison said.

Reese eyed him up and down. "Maybe I need something to interact with, *honey*. And I don't mean a platter full of moussaka."

Hopping onstage, Mr. Levin pulled Reese aside. He liked to keep his comments private with each actor, but Harrison could make out a phrase here and there: "It's an ensemble piece . . . give and take . . . too late for surprises . . ." Reese was not taking it well. From the expression on her face, she looked as if he were telling her to wear curlers and sing in Swedish.

Then, with a barely audible *fwoomp*, the entire auditorium went black.

All conversation stopped.

"Dashiell?" Mr. Levin called out. "What happened?"

"Sorry, I was testing the override!" Dashiell cried from the projection booth. "I'll set it back . . . wait. Aw, *scheiss*. It froze."

"Who can unfreeze it?" Brianna shouted. "I thought we had a Wi-Fi setup—"

"Casey!" Mr. Levin cried out. "CASEY!"

"I'll find her," Harrison said. As he groped his way across the nearly pitch-black stage, his hands met something soft and yielding about chest-high.

"Harrison!" Reese said in a shocked voice.

"You did that on purpose," Harrison replied.

"CASEY!!!"

Casey heard her name from out in the hallway. She grabbed her bag of baked chips from the vending machine and ran. What could have gone wrong now? Everything was going wrong. Today was dress rehearsal. Everything was supposed to go right!

She burst through a side door into blackness. A flashlight beam caught her in the eye, and a hand closed around her left arm. "It's me, the Phantom of the Opera," Charles said. "You need to override the override, or something. Or reprogram Dashiell's flake-o-meter."

Casey's laptop was glowing just inside the main curtain. She carefully made her way there and saw what Dashiell had done. The override was something he had programmed as a kind of exercise. A method of setting the entire cue sheet on automatic. Which made no sense. She quickly reset the cues to manual and cued the houselights.

"Thank you!" Dashiell called out.

"Casey, where were you?" Mr. Levin said, rushing toward her. "This is *dress*. We're running twenty-five minutes late. How can we time this show if you're wandering away?"

Casey put her bag of chips behind her back. "Sorry . . . "

"Maybe we should just put the snack machine back here," Reese said. "Then we won't lose Casey so often."

"Knock it off, Tinkerbell," Charles said.

"Reese? Brianna and I would like to work with you briefly on that last number, alone," Mr. Levin said, heading back onto the stage. "Places!"

"Delighted," Reese replied. As she turned to follow him, she winked at Kyle.

Kyle ambled backstage, shaking his head. "She is something, huh? I'm sitting there minding my own business and whoops! Hello! Kyle boldly goes where no man has gone before."

"I doubt *that*," Charles said.

As Charles bustled back to the big room, Kyle stood next to Casey, watching Reese. Casey was silent. She felt the desperate urge for chips and took a fistful. She hadn't talked to Kyle since the night in the village green.

And she hadn't stopped eating.

She should have been over it by now. Kyle had said hi to her every day in school, he had smiled at her—like nothing was wrong. Like the night in the park was just a friendly walk and not the most amazing night of her life. Like he hadn't turned her upside down and then shot off to the village green to do the same thing with Reese.

She hadn't told him that she'd seen him. She had just frozen him out, hoping he would notice. The most infuriating thing was that he hadn't.

Who else had he done this with? What percentage of the school belonged to Kyle's private friends-with-benefits club? Or had he settled on Reese for the long term—just used Casey as an appetizer?

Reese was all over the stage, singing her number with such a huge self-satisfied grin that you would think she'd just been given a one-woman show.

"Hey, Case," Kyle said casually. "Too bad Mr. Michaels doesn't come here every day, huh?"

"Mm-hm."

" 'Sup?"

"Nothing," Casey said.

"What's the matter? Are you mad at me?"

Will miracles never cease?

She wasn't nervous anymore. Nothing about him made her nervous now. She calmly took her headphones off and draped them on her shoulders. "That night? After we . . . you know," Casey said. "I saw you and Reese."

"Oh," Kyle said, his smile drooping. "No wonder you've been so quiet."

"So the answer is, yeah, I'm mad . . ."

"Reese and I had this plan," Kyle said defensively. "We were going to meet after Brianna's party. Reese said she wanted to talk about a new idea for the play. She said she had to go home first, because her parents are jerks about her staying out late, so she had to pretend to go to sleep and then sneak out. I didn't know . . . okay, maybe I suspected . . . I'm stupider than I look, I guess . . . and, well, *you* know Reese . . ."

Casey hadn't been this close to Kyle since that night, and her body was reacting, drinking him up greedily. But he wasn't the same guy she'd thought he was then. He couldn't be. She'd made him into something larger than just Kyle. Into some kind of God figure, Father Confessor, boyfriend, lover, all rolled into one. Part of her was still seeing him that way, and neither she nor he deserved that.

"I'm not really mad the way you think I am," Casey said, trying to get it clear in her own mind. "Okay, yeah, my feelings were hurt when I saw you and Reese. But not as much as I thought they would be. The weirdest thing happened, Kyle. It was like my mind saw all the usual things it would be expected to do—scream, explode, cry, freak—but I wasn't really feeling angry enough to do any of those things. I was, like, full of *relief*."

"Relief?" Kyle said. He looked baffled and maybe a little hurt.

"Look, I *knew* you had plans with someone else, Kyle.

You'd told me so. That was your business. But I also realized you didn't have to go looking for me after that party. No one else did—just you. I needed someone so badly, Kyle. Someone to talk to, someone who would let me be confused and try to untangle my life. And despite your plans, you listened and asked questions and tried to make me feel good. You did make me feel good. You were kind. I don't know too many guys who are kind. For the first time I felt safe enough to open up. I'd kept everything back for so long behind lies and silence, and there it was, spilling out. Everything went so fast, and I felt so raw and emotional. Everything we did after that—it was *natural*. I knew you weren't faking, or trying to manipulate me. I enjoyed it, Kyle. Even if it didn't mean what I might have wanted it to mean."

Kyle took it all in. "I haven't told anyone, you know."

"I know," Casey said. "Thanks for that. Anyway, I learned something. I want to tell people about the accident. I have to. At the right time. After the show. I didn't think I ever would, but now I know I will."

"Casey?" Kyle said, struggling to find words. "Since that night I've wanted to tell you—"

"Cue three-seventy-two A and B—COME IN, CASEY, THAT'S YOUR CUE, YOU'RE LATE!" Mr. Levin's voice crackled over her headphones.

"Oh, my God." Casey slid the phones back over her ears and ran to her console. The musical number had just ended, and Reese had jumped down from the piano. The scene-change cue was late. The turntable was supposed to move, and a flat was supposed to be lowered in the dark.

"Hel-*lo*?" came Reese's voice from the stage.

Casey's laptop screen glowed a red "late" warning. She quickly pressed the enter key, and the warning disappeared. The turntable motor began to hum.

"Whoooa—what the *hell?*" Reese was tottering, off balance. She windmilled her arms, one of which hit the piano with a loud smack.

Screaming, she fell to the floor. She tried to get up but couldn't. Her costume had somehow gotten stuck in the turntable groove.

"CASEY!" Mr. Levin shouted. "CANCEL THE CUE!"

Frantically Casey tried to hit the control-alt-delete key combination, but her fingers felt like toes.

From above she heard another familiar hum.

The flat.

It was a backdrop for a new scene, nearly the width of the stage. A huge wooden-framed canvas with a steel bar across the bottom. It was supposed to lower slowly from above when everyone was off the stage. Now its massive frame came into sight just at the same time the turntable was moving Reese directly underneath it.

Casey's fingers were grimy and shaking, slipping on the keyboard as if she'd never used it.

The flat connected with Reese's right shoulder, hard, and she shrieked.

21

"DO SOMETHING!" BRIANNA SCREAMED.

She ran onto the stage and pushed aside the clot of people around Reese. Reese was on the floor, pinned by the flat. She had managed to get her hands underneath it and was struggling to push it away, but it was way too heavy. Its weight kept her nearly motionless while the turntable continued to move beneath her, pulling at her. Mr. Levin was trying to lift the flat and Brianna joined him.

"*You're hurting me!*" Reese wailed.

"Push!" Mr. Levin said. Now Ms. Gunderson, Charles, Harrison, Vijay, and Kyle had wrapped their hands under the frame. "One . . . two . . . three . . . "

They lifted. The flat rose a few inches, and Brianna pulled Reese free. As they all fell back, the rumbling turntable motor stopped—and as slowly as it came down, the flat rose again.

Casey stepped out from behind the curtain. Her face was ashen.

"A little late," Reese said through gritted teeth.

"How do you feel?" Mr. Levin asked, kneeling beside her.

"Can you move your upper body?" Harrison asked.

Reese grimaced at Harrison. "Maybe you should help me find out."

"She's fine," Charles said with a laugh.

"I'll call the school nurse," Ms. Gunderson said.

Mr. Levin and Ms. Gunderson helped Reese to her feet. She was testing all the parts of her body like a dancer, doing little isolation movements. Brianna looked up into the fly space. The flat was enormous. The fact that Reese got her hands underneath it was probably what had saved her from more serious injury.

"I'm all right," Reese said, moving her injured arm in a circle. "I'll probably get a big ugly hideous bruise . . . but the costume will cover it."

Casey was staring at them from the side of the stage. She looked frightened, as if she were about to cry. "I'm so sorry . . . "

"Do those headphones work, Casey?" Mr. Levin called out.

"Yes," Casey squeaked.

Brianna could tell Mr. Levin was furious. But now that Reese was all right, his teacher instincts were taking over. "The show opens tomorrow, and this kind of thing cannot happen. I would like an ironclad reassurance."

"It won't happen," Casey said.

"Let's run the rest of the show—Reese, you can mark it, take it easy—and if I see one cue even *partially* late, I'm canceling all performances. Casey, I will see you after rehearsal."

An hour later the hallways were silent. Casey sat spread-legged on the shiny floor, listening to the distant whir of a vacuum cleaner, thinking about what might have been. Reese could have been seriously hurt. The flat was humongous. Had she been an inch farther, it might have come down on her head.

Mr. Levin had cooled off a bit by the time he lectured her after the rehearsal. But Casey knew what she had done was unforgivable. It could have been much worse. She hadn't been paying attention. She'd been too wrapped up in Kyle and her personal life.

Kara Chang of Westfield, Connecticut, was all about dedication and concentration. She would have fixed the problem long ago. But Casey Chang was different—way too often she was scared and tentative, like a person with a layer of skin peeled off.

Before the talk with Kyle, Casey hadn't really understood all this. Now she saw it clearly. She understood why she had made this mistake. She had jumped into this position too early. She hadn't been ready to be a person again, let alone a stage manager. No wonder Brianna had been so pissed at her. Brianna forced you to be yourself, like it or not. And Casey hadn't been able to do that. Her self had been buried too deep.

She needed time to dig it out. Time to let a scab form over the shock and grief. To rebuild her trust in herself, so that eventually others could trust her, too. To do nothing except the quiet, normal things. To heal.

She could still get that time. But a person had to give to get. And there was one thing she needed to do.

With careful penmanship, Casey finished up her note. Charles was still inside with the Charlettes, Harrison, and Brianna. Everyone else had left.

Dear Mr. Levin, Ms. Gunderson, and the DC,

First of all, I want to apologize for my mistake. I am so sorry for what happened—Reese, please forgive me. There is no excuse for what I did.

Second, I just want you to know I care about this fantastic play very much and I have made every contribution I could. My only goal has always been to help. So it is with deep thought that I have decided the best thing to do is resign, effective immediately. Dashiell will run the cues much better than I could do, and Charles and the Charlettes will easily pick up the other chores.

These have been two of the most wonderful months of my life. I hope I gave you half as much as you all gave me.

Break a leg. I love you.

Sincerely,

Casey Chang

If she read it one more time, she was going to break out crying.

She signed it, folded it, and put it in an envelope.

The theater was eerily quiet as she walked inside and onto the stage. The houselights were on, and Casey stood there looking at the seats, soaking it in for the last time. From behind her a tune began. Cold Play. "You Belong to Me." It was coming from the costume/prop room.

She stepped backstage and peeked inside. Charles, Harrison, Brianna, Vijay, and a couple of other Charlettes were sitting at the table. The Afro wigs, which had arrived today, were on the top shelf, the only place they fit. In the center of the table was Charles's iPod, playing the music on a docking station. On the floor were two buckets full of shiny sequins.

Everyone was sewing sequins onto shirts and pants. As the garments moved, the wall sparkled with light. "What's this?" Casey asked.

"Costumes for the final scene," Charles said.

"But the cast doesn't change costumes for that scene," Casey said.

"It does now." Harrison smiled. "We close the show with 'You Are the Light of the World.' We're supposed to send everyone home with hope and happiness."

"And what says hope and happiness more than sequins?" Charles said with a shrug. He had drawn plans and laid them on the table. The vests were all broad shoulders and angles, ablaze with light.

Casey fiddled with her envelope. "I—I have something I wanted to show you," she said.

"What is it?" Charles asked distractedly.

"You, um, have to read it," she said.

Charles held out a needle and thread. "Can it wait?" he asked. "We need another seamstress here."

The Cold Play song ended and a soft, haunting recording of "Amazing Grace" began.

"Amazing grace, how sweet the sound,
That saved a wretch like me.
I once was lost, but now I'm found,
Was blind, but now I see."

One by one, the Drama Club members began to sing harmony. Casey heard a sweet, strong voice lift over the others and realized it was the first time she had heard Brianna sing. She was wonderful.

Brianna looked up, deep in thought, and smiled. It was the first time she had smiled at Casey in a week. Maybe a mistake, maybe she was thinking about something else. But it felt good.

The vests were taking shape. The room glowed and hummed. Casey took it all in. It had been a long two months. She was a different person now than on that first day. The Drama Club felt like family to her.

The room felt like home.

Casey folded her envelope, put it in her pocket, and began to sew.

22

From: <dramakween312@rport.li.com>
To: <rkolodzny@yaleuniversity.edu>
Subject: AAAAAAAAAAA
November 16, 5:07 P.M.

rachel

oh my god. IT'S OPENING NIGHT!!!!

    i am reduced to writing in all capitals with multiple exclamation points and feeling like someone out of a disney movie and living all the show-biz cliches in the world because that's what it's like, and no matter what you do or who you are YOU CAN'T HELP BUT FEEL IT!!!!

    the wigs r here. the canes r here. they finally got

delivered to the right address. u would not believe the costumes for the final number. reese's shoulder is bruised and she can't be quite as flamboyant with that arm, but that's probably all for the best (do i hear a song? ☺). kyle's ankle is almost back to normal. harrison is smiling. mr. levin is smiling. ms. gunderson is smiling at mr. levin. IT'S ALL WORKING OUT!

WISH YOU WERE HERE!!!!!!

Mr. Levin's face went pale when Harrison told everyone the news. "What do you mean, Lori can't make it?" he said. "We're going up tonight! She *has* to!"

"Is it the flu?" Ms. Gunderson asked.

"It's her parents," Harrison explained. He could barely get the words out. Lori had called him just this afternoon, a half hour after school. She hadn't shown up in the auditorium for brushups. When she told him the reason, he thought it was a joke at first. "That time she said she was sick? It wasn't because she wanted to postpone her parents' conferences. She wanted to avoid any contact between us and them. They had no idea she was involved in this show. She told them she was staying after school for tutoring. They only found out the truth today, when they saw her script."

"Why didn't she just tell them?" Reese asked. "What's the big deal?"

Harrison shook his head. "They went through the roof when they found out. They think the script is blasphemy. Christ in a Superman shirt, songs with sexy lyrics, clown paint on the disciples' faces—they have a whole list of reasons."

"You've got to be kidding," Brianna said. "*Godspell* is so mainstream. Where have they been since 1972?"

"Have you Googled *Godspell*?" Dashiell asked. "I've seen this kind of stuff. People quoting scripture, foaming at the mouth. To some people, it's still very controversial."

"Lori was in tears," Harrison said. "She could barely speak. She kept defending them, telling me not to be mad, saying it was all her fault for leaving the script around."

"I say we march over there and pull her away," Brianna said. "Bring a TV news crew if we have to. Make them look like Neanderthals in public. They don't own her. She's a senior! She's eighteen!"

"Sixteen," Charles corrected her. "She skipped fourth grade, and her birthday is in November."

Mr. Levin was pacing back and forth. "We're not going to win this battle," he said. "Look, people have different religious beliefs. This is America. If the parents say no, and the child obeys their wishes, there's not much we can do. And I know those parents. They do not yield."

"Oh, please . . . " Reese murmured.

"It's the biggest female part in the show!" Casey piped up. "We can't go on without her."

Mr. Levin exhaled heavily. Harrison couldn't see the expression behind the glasses. "Yes, Casey. You're right. We can't."

Harrison's cell phone was still in his right hand. He only now realized how tight his fingers had closed around it. His knuckles were white. He had the urge to throw it, to smash it against the wall, then grind the pieces to silicone dust beneath his shoes. This was beyond belief. All the hours, the days of preparation, the songs and lines and comic bits practiced to perfection, the friendships cemented and nearly lost, the gleaming Cyclone fence and hand-sewn vests—wasted!

He looked up into a circle of pallid, stunned faces. Charles had one arm around Brianna and the other around Dashiell, whose glasses were starting to fog up. Casey had begun to cry, and Kyle was pounding his right fist into his left hand.

"I—I was really looking forward to this," Harrison said.

"I'll make a cancellation announcement for whoever is still in school," Mr. Levin said. "Casey, can you get out an e-mail blast to the parent list, with a high-priority flag?"

Casey nodded. Wiping her eyes, she turned toward her laptop.

"Maybe when Lori's parents see that," Charles said, "they'll come to their senses."

But Casey's fingers hovered motionlessly over the keyboard. Slowly she shut the top. "I'm not going to send an e-mail."

Harrison looked at her blankly. "You think we should do a phone tree?"

"We can't do a phone tree," Mr. Levin said wearily. "There's simply not enough time and too many families."

"I think we should go on," Casey said simply.

The place fell silent.

"Um, Casey?" Harrison said with a weary sigh. "Let's be real."

"Brianna knows the part," Casey declared.

Brianna's face drained of color. She stared at Casey, stunned.

"Brianna has never *done* the part," Harrison said.

"She's been watching every rehearsal," Casey said. "She has a photographic memory. She's been singing these songs since she was a little girl, and she's seen the movie . . . how many times, Bri?"

"Seventeen," Brianna said softly.

"What do you say, then?" Casey asked.

Everyone stared at Brianna, who swallowed hard. "I— well, yeah. I mean, I do know the lines, I think . . . "

"Yyyyes!" Kyle shouted, pumping the air with his fist.

"Wait a minute!" Mr. Levin said, shaking his head. "We rehearsed Lori for weeks—blocking, lines, songs. Curtain is at seven-thirty. It's four-thirty now. We would have three hours to do what we did in all those weeks. The idea is noble but impractical. Brianna, you are supremely talented, but—"

"Three hours." Casey held up her clipboard and began writing. "The lines and blocking in the spoken scenes are most important. We'll run them first. I can skip chunks of dialogue where Lori has no lines, and we'll cut to cues. Songs are not as important because Brianna knows them cold. We'll call the orchestra in after the dialogue and run Brianna's solo, then a cue-to-cue *only* on all the other songs, to save time. I figure if we can stay on task and stagger the dinner break, we'll be done before half hour at seven."

Reese's jaw dropped. "Wow. Did you just think of that?"

"Sounds like a plan," Harrison said.

"If Brianna says she can do the role, she can," Dashiell said.

"Charles, what about the costumes?" Casey asked.

Charles eyed Brianna carefully. "Here a dart, there a dart, everywhere a dart, dart. Easy enough."

"Please?" Reese said. "Please please please please please please?"

"What do you say, Greg?" Ms. Gunderson asked.

Mr. Levin took off his glasses and mopped his brow. With a grim expression, he looked at the wall clock.

"I say, skip dinner and start from the top."

Never say never. . . . If at first you don't succeed, you weren't trying hard enough. . . . A baseball player who fails to get on base seven times out of ten is still a star. . . . Brianna had lived by those rules all her life.

She was an idiot.

"Hold still!" Charles said, his teeth clamped around pins as he hemmed a pair of jeans she was wearing.

Vijay was fiddling with her hair. "Lori had the ponytail. But it's the wrong hair color now."

"Screw the ponytail!"

"But the people from the shop will be in the audience, and they'll expect to see it," Vijay said. "They didn't charge us for it."

"Then *you* wear it!" Charles snapped.

"Brianna? You have a line here!" Casey said.

If Charles hadn't put a tight flannel shirt on her, Brianna's heart might have burst from her chest. How could she recite lines with the Charlettes pinching and pulling and touching, Casey watching her like a horse trainer with a stopwatch, and the cast members speeding through lines as if on fast-forward?

"LINE!" she screamed. "Give me the line!"

She *thought* she knew them. She could picture Lori saying *something*. But it was as if Lori had stolen the words and taken them home with her. Photographic memory? Forget it.

Mr. Levin jogged onstage and gave the script to her. "You don't need a prompter, Brianna, you need this. Look, even if you have to hold it during the performance, it's okay. I've seen professional actors do it in last-minute emergencies like this. Audiences are very forgiving. They root for the underdog. You'll probably get a standing ovation."

Oh, right, Brianna thought. *She can't do the job, so we bank on the sympathy vote.* Using a script in a performance was pathetic. Like doing the whole show with a rip up the back of your costume. "Thanks but no thanks," she said.

Casey raced to her side and took her by the arm. "Take the script," she said firmly. "It will calm you down. You know more than you think."

"This was your idea, Casey—"

"And it's a good one. You're going to save the day." As Casey headed back into the wings, she shouted to the other actors: "Say the lines at the normal speed, guys. Act like it's a performance and take it from the top!"

Brianna obeyed. She read directly from the page. Her eyes would instinctively dart ahead, over the familiar dialogue. Somehow, *seeing* the lines made a huge difference. It was like digging them out of a deep hiding place. By the end of the dialogue run-through she was maybe 70 percent off-book. Which may have been great for a baseball player, but it still sucked for an actor.

"We have to move on," Casey said. "We're running ahead of schedule, though, so I'll run lines with you after we do the songs. Dashiell, are you set with the lights?"

"Roger," came Dashiell's voice from the booth.

"Musicians, take it from the top!" Casey commanded. " 'Day by Day'!"

As the five-piece band started, Brianna cleared her throat. This was the biggest and most famous number in the show. Lori always nailed it each time.

" 'Day by daaaay . . . ' " Brianna began.

She sounded like Prince in his squeaky phase. She could barely get above a whisper, no matter how hard she tried. Her long extended "daaaaay" sounded like "deh." "Death" without the "th."

"It's too low!" she finally shouted in the middle of the song.

"You sound fine," Kyle said.

"That's because you're right in front of me!" Brianna said.

"Dashielllll!" Casey shouted. "Turn up the body mike!"

"It's as high as it'll go!" he replied. "We'll blow out the system."

"Let's just try it again," Ms. Gunderson said. "Band? *One*-two-three, *one*-two three . . . "

The music began. Brianna wanted to explode. This wasn't going to work.

"Stop!" she shouted. "STOP! This was the worst idea ever."

Barely holding back tears, she stormed off the stage.

23

"BRIANNA!" CASEY CALLED OUT, HER VOICE dying in the dry autumn night air. *"Brianna, stop!"*

She was out of breath when she caught up to her on Porterfield Avenue. "Are you okay?"

"Did you e-mail the parents?" Brianna snapped, not breaking stride.

"No," Casey said as she tried to keep pace.

"Then it seems you have a job to do."

"Come on, Brianna. Look, you were good. *So* good. I know you can do it. You're a total pro."

"A professional moron."

"What is it? Are you comparing your voice to Lori's? It's different. Yours is just as fun to listen to. I thought the rehearsal was going well."

"Well, I think I suck," Brianna said. "This wasn't my idea, it was yours, Casey. You got us into this mess, and if I were you, I would not want to be responsible for an audience full of parents showing up when there's no show *on account of religious reasons!*"

"Brianna, I don't *think* you can do a great job, I know it. Okay, so maybe you won't be one hundred and two percent perfect, but who is? Kyle is still figuring out his right foot from his left. Do you think anyone cares? This is such an opportunity, Brianna. You thought you couldn't act because you were student directing. And now? You can save the show. You can prevent everyone's work from being wasted. Your picture will be on the Wall. No one will ever forget this, Brianna. Especially me."

Brianna stopped and looked right into Casey's eyes. "I live for this club. I have since long before you got here. When it looked like we had to fold, and you suggested I do the role, I agreed for the sake of the group. I tried to pull this show out of a hat. I put my ass on the line, and I have every right to take it back. I know when I can or can't handle something, Casey. I know who I am. And if you know who you are, you'll get out of my face and be a responsible stage manager."

Casey wasn't expecting that. She felt suddenly short of breath. "Well, I guess we're very different people," was all she could think to say.

"We *are* different, Casey." Brianna's face was fiery red. "I like things out in the open. I like it when my friends know everything about me. I *don't* like it when they do things behind my back."

"Behind your . . . ?" Casey had to reach deep inside

for this one, to switch gears from the play. This was about Kyle. The play was on the line, and they were out here arguing about *Kyle*! "Um, Brianna, do you think I tried to steal Kyle from you? Do you think Kyle cares about you anyway? Or me? No offense, Brianna, but he doesn't. Not either of us. Just Reese."

"Duh. It wasn't for lack of trying, though, was it?"

"Do you really want to know what happened between Kyle and me? Because I'll tell you right now—"

"Spare me the details. This is more than just about Kyle, Casey. It's about hiding things. And keeping secrets. About not letting in the people who care about you. It's always been about that, Casey."

"What are you talking about?"

"*I don't know.* You tell me, Casey. I'm not stupid and I'm not blind. *What are you hiding?*"

Casey took a deep breath. She looked up the long expanse of Porterfield Avenue toward the front of the school, an absurdly grand columned entrance to a boxy building that looked empty and desolate.

She looked at her watch. Six thirty-five. Her cell phone was vibrating. This was pushing it.

"Okay," Casey said. "You're right. I do have a few things to tell you."

"Make it fast. It's cold out here."

"First of all, I'm sorry I yelled at you," Casey said. "Second of all, my name isn't Casey . . ."

Harrison watched Kyle lope around the stage, making ape noises, then drop to the floor and do thirty push-ups at breakneck speed, then leap as high as his ankle allowed a few times. This was followed by a repeated nasal "Meow meow meow meow . . ." starting in a falsetto and traveling down the scale into the lowest bass range of his voice. Harrison had taught him all these exercises during the rehearsal process, but he'd never once seen Kyle doing them.

The truth was, Kyle didn't need the exercises. He was doing them because he was nervous. He didn't need that either. His life was about to change, big-time, and he wouldn't know what hit him.

Harrison brushed some lint off his costume and adjusted the suspenders. Everyone else was running around like crazy, crying and jabbering and shaking and whispering into one another's ears. Reese had pulled her top down over her right shoulder so Charles could smear it with Tiger Balm, nearly exposing her breast and angling herself for the maximum attention to that detail. The ointment made the whole place smell like a locker room.

In a moment it all faded to nothing.

Mr. Levin was in front of the curtain. Harrison could hear him tapping the mike and saying, "Testing, testing."

He felt a sharp pinch on his butt and didn't have to turn around to know it was Reese. He slapped at her hand blindly, without looking, and made contact. Good reflexes.

"Ow," Reese said.

"Ladies and gentlemen," Mr. Levin announced, "I want to thank you for coming out on this cold night. I have an announcement to make. I wish we could have told you earlier, but we found out only this evening.

Unfortunately, Lori Terrell cannot be with us tonight."

There must have been a lot of kids in the audience, because Kyle could hear them murmuring their disappointment.

"Instead," Mr. Levin went on, "her role will be played by Brianna Glaser."

A smattering of applause filtered in before Mr. Levin shouted, "So let's give it up for *Godspell!*"

For a moment Harrison felt as if something were completely wrong. Like he couldn't breathe and his arms were numb. Like if he moved, he would crumple to the floor as if he'd been sacked by the entire defensive line of the RHS football team. "Breathe," he heard Brianna whisper behind him. She emerged from the darkness, smiling, and squeezed his hand. At the opposite side of the stage, he could see Charles shooting everyone a thumbs-up with one hand and wiping his eyes with the other.

They were feelings he had before every show. He smiled. It was right.

The music began, and Harrison felt a palm clasping the back of his neck. "I kick left first?" a familiar voice asked. "In 'All for the Best'?"

"Right first," Harrison whispered. "*Right.*"

"Right," Kyle said. "I'll never remember it."

"Well, break a leg, brother," Harrison said as he stepped forward onto the stage. He hit his mark, a blue masking-tape X on the floor, as the curtain opened and a spotlight set him ablaze.

24

HE WAS A PHENOMENON.

Not just good. Not just talented.

He seemed to suck energy from the walls and give it back a thousand times. The audience ate him up, cheering his every entrance.

For all the impressive stuff Kyle had done in rehearsal, nothing had prepared Harrison for being onstage with someone like this. The pressure of performance did something to him. It was hard to compete with, but God was it fun.

"Places for 'All for the Best,' " came Casey's voice from backstage.

Harrison braced himself. He had taped his shins in advance. Kyle's eyes, crisp and confident until that moment, flickered with uncertainty.

Harrison caught a glimpse of Charles and the

Charlettes, all holding hands backstage as if in prayer.

Sure. *They* didn't have to worry about injury.

The music began, and the two guys sang their verse. Kyle's voice was robust and clear. Together they hopped onto the platform, and Kyle shot him a panicked glance.

Great. Kyle was "up." He had blanked out on what to do.

Harrison panicked. He was singing—he couldn't tell Kyle where to kick. *Why couldn't he remember this?* Harrison would have to indicate some other way, with some other part of his body.

Eyes. Wink with the eye on the side of the body where the leg should kick.

In the middle of the verse, Harrison winked with one eye. Kyle nodded imperceptibly.

And Harrison realized he had winked *left.*

Out came the hats. And the canes. Harrison desperately tried to get Kyle to look at him again. He couldn't fall in the middle of this number. Not on opening night.

"And . . . kickline . . ." Reese mouthed from backstage.

Harrison kicked right. He closed his eyes instinctively. *Brace . . . just brace . . .*

Applause welled up from the audience. And Harrison noticed his shin felt fine.

Kyle was doing it. Kicking right. Swinging his cane left and kicking like a friggin' Rockette!

They swung and kicked and sang like clockwork, and at the end of the number they fell into each other, arms around shoulders, tipping their hats in grand vaudeville style. The crowd roared and made them take two bows.

"We did it!" Kyle said as they lowered their heads together. "Woo-HOO! Thanks for that wink."

Harrison smiled and kept his mouth shut.

" . . . the light of the world!"

Brianna held the final position. The tableau. With their arms spread and Dashiell's special lighting, the sequins shot color around the theater like an explosion. It had all happened so fast, she wasn't sure what she'd just experienced. Was it over? Could it possibly be over?

The silence after the last note was total. Dashiell cut the lights, and the entire theater was black. Like the world had been whisked away, leaving them all hovering in outer space.

And then, after what felt like a decade, the noise began.

She expected to hear clapping, but that wasn't what came first. It was a roar, a wash of voices across the width and depth of the theater like the boom of an airplane breaking the sound barrier.

The lights came on again. Brianna relaxed her muscles, dropped her pose. She felt Harrison's hands gripping hers. She reached out and took Jamil's. The cast fanned out across the apron of the stage and stood there as the audience gave and gave, screaming, clapping, shouting the names of the cast members. Harrison nodded, and they all took a bow.

Then, one by one according to plan, they stepped forward for individual bows. "When do I go?" Brianna asked Jamil, nearly shouting to be heard above the applause.

"You're after me!" he replied, kissing her exuberantly on the cheek. "You were *amazing!*"

When her turn came, she stepped forward. She wasn't

prepared for what happened. The entire audience rose up as if on cue, crowding the airspace, yelling and whistling and hooting so loud she thought maybe Kyle had snuck out behind her and they were applauding *him*.

But he hadn't. It was for her, and for the first time in front of a live audience, she cried.

They stayed on their feet for Harrison's bow. His applause was huge, too, for a powerful performance — and when Kyle finally came to center stage, dramatically spinning his cape, an ear-piercing squeal went up from a huge group of girls in the back rows, and what must have been the entire football team chanted "WOO! WOO! WOO! WOO!"

Kyle bowed and tried to move back into line, but Harrison pushed him forward again.

He was a rock star.

Brianna shot a look toward Casey at backstage right, whose face was drenched in tears of joy. She had the urge to run back there, to drag her onstage, but found herself wrapped tightly in Harrison's strong arms. "You were sensational," he said.

"*Vre* Harrison," Brianna replied. "So were you."

He smiled. "We did it, sister. We pulled it off."

They separated for one more group bow, with Kyle in the center, all holding hands to keep from floating into the wings.

"Who's your daddy?" Dashiell shrieked, gyrating backstage with a headset dangling from his neck.

"WOOOO-HOOOO!" Casey bounced from hug to

hug, screaming and crying and vowing love and loyalty forever and basically saying whatever came into her head because the show had worked, it had been nearly flawless, and she had earned the right to say whatever she wanted.

"Caseyyyyy . . . " Brianna said, standing center stage behind the closed curtain with her arms wide and her face makeup dripping black rivulets down her cheeks. The two girls shared an embrace that shut out the world for a moment. "Thank you. Thank you so much for believing in me. Thank you for *putting up* with me. I'm *so* glad you pushed me, Casey."

"You were perfect, Brianna. Not one mistake—"

"Three."

"Okay, three. But no one noticed."

"All right, girls, break it up, break it up!" Charles shouted, clapping his hands. "We have another performance tomorrow night, and we're already losing sequins."

"*Chaaaaarles!*" The two girls mauled him, wrapping him in hugs from either side.

"Aaaaghhh!" Charles screamed. "Help! I'm being mmphmphmrrrphlrg!"

The next few minutes passed in a blur of hugs and kisses, traveling from backstage to hallway, from ecstatic cast to ecstatic families and friends—and finally they were all in the dressing rooms, peeling off clothing with a recklessness for the material that nearly gave Charles a coronary, and then into their party clothes and makeup.

They all swept out of the school, traveling in a wave to Ivy's, the upscale Chinese restaurant where the traditional cast parties for the big shows were held. Ivy, as always, had promised to set aside a section of the restaurant for food and dancing.

Twenty minutes later, the music was cranked up, and Brianna screamed at the top of her lungs, boogying as if she hadn't just had the most difficult day of her life.

Casey bounced from person to person, giggling and laughing. Someone put a diamond tiara on her head, probably swiped from the costume room, and someone else gave her a pair of rhinestone glasses and a feather boa. She waved it around, wrapping other people together with her.

"Go, Casey!" Brianna screamed.

Reese, dancing her perfect jazz dance moves, sidled over and smiled. "Some of us are going to the beach. Wanna come?"

"Sure," Brianna said. "Who are we going with?"

Reese shrugged. "I have *my* ride. I'm sure you'll find one."

She nodded toward the front door. There, Kyle was talking to a group of admirers. He was wearing a black leather jacket. His hair was swept back, and he looked about as sexy as was humanly possible.

Casey suddenly felt cold. She could sense Brianna stiffening.

Oh Lord, this wasn't over, was it? It still was all about Kyle....

"See you there, girls." Reese yawned theatrically and began strutting across the throng of bodies toward Kyle.

At the other end of the restaurant, Kyle threw his head back, laughing. As Reese danced her way through the bodies, waving to get Kyle's attention, he put his arm around a blond sophomore whose name Casey didn't know. The girl rested her head on Kyle's shoulder, and they both headed for the exit, their bodies leaning into each other, walking in lockstep.

Reese stopped in her tracks. Her shoulders drooped.

Casey looked at Brianna. "Unbelievable," she murmured.

"Kyle!" Reese's voice echoed over the crowd. "KYYYYYLLLLE!"

Brianna's face broke first. Then Casey couldn't help herself, an undignified "HAAAA!" escaping from her mouth as she leaned into Brianna, both of them convulsed and holding on to each other and crying with laughter, and Casey felt as if her rib cage were going to split open.

Wiping her eyes, Brianna continued to dance. She whirled around, threading in and out of Charles and Aisha, Dashiell and Becky, Jamil and Lynnette. And Casey.

Ivy had just opened the buffet, and a line was forming. But Brianna didn't care. She couldn't stop dancing. The night was young. The year was young. There would be plenty of time for food.

Plenty of time for everything.

Epilogue

WE SNUCK BACK IN TO THE SCHOOL AFTER the party, Brianna and I. Mr. Ippolito was still there, cleaning up with his crew. We headed straight for the Shrine. Arm in arm, we stood in front of the photos and looked at them a long time. It was the most amazing thing. They looked different. As if the people in them had changed. I saw *everybody*. Charles was in 1957, I forget the play. Dashiell showed up in *Kiss Me, Kate* from 1979, and Reese — well, for some reason she was there four different times.

Once again I was stumped looking for myself. Brianna kept suggesting things, but I rejected them. You have to *know*. You have to feel it in your gut. I thought maybe I would see myself in a character who had undergone some huge transformation. Annie Oakley or Molly Brown or Sarah Brown or Lady Macbeth or Ophelia or Juliet. But none of them felt right. Brianna was getting frustrated with me, so I gave up.

It was when I started walking away that the girl spotted me.

There she was, peeking out of a photo on the lower left. Not in any meaningful play at all. Just the chorus of a production of *Brigadoon*. She wasn't Asian, either, just a plain white girl in a Scottish-looking outfit dancing a jig. The lead guys, returning to the real world, have crossed the bridge, which means (in the plot) that they're about to destroy the dreamland of *Brigadoon*.

The guys are in focus, but the chorus is blurry. I don't remember noticing that the first time. I don't know if that was done on purpose in the dark room or if it's just a trick of perspective.

And then I saw that the girl in the center of the chorus was crystal clear. As I passed, her eyes went with me. Her expression was steady and secure, as if she knew she would stay there while everything around her was fading.

I don't know why I thought she was me. Honestly, the image kind of shocked me. I didn't tell Brianna. At first I figured she wouldn't understand, or would disagree. Or maybe I'd even change my own mind. But after I went home that night, I couldn't stop thinking about her.

I still can't. And I still see her and say hi to her every day.

I haven't told anyone yet. And she hasn't faded a bit.